THE UNFINISHED HOUSE

DATE DUE

GAYLORD   PRINTED IN U S.A.

A JUDY BOLTON Mystery

The Unfinished House

BY
Margaret Sutton

Illustrated by Pelagic Doane

APPLEWOOD BOOKS
Bedford, Massachusetts

The Unfinished House
was originally published in 1938.

Reprinted by permission of the estate of Margaret Sutton.
All Rights Reserved.

For a complete list of titles in the Judy Bolton Mysteries,
please visit judybolton.awb.com.

Thank you for purchasing an Applewood Book.
Applewood reprints America's lively classics—books from
the past that are still of interest to modern readers.
For a free copy of our current catalog, write to:

Applewood Books
P.O. Box 365
Bedford, MA 01730
www.awb.com

ISBN 978-1-4290-9031-5

MANUFACTURED IN THE U.S.A.

"ARTHUR THINKS WE'LL HAVE TROUBLE," JUDY
VENTURED.

A JUDY BOLTON MYSTERY

THE UNFINISHED HOUSE

BY
MARGARET SUTTON

AUTHOR OF
THE HAUNTED ATTIC,
THE MAGIC MAKERS, ETC.

ILLUSTRATED BY
PELAGIE DOANE

GROSSET & DUNLAP
PUBLISHERS   NEW YORK

To Peggy,
My Little Helper

JUDY BOLTON
MYSTERY STORIES

By MARGARET SUTTON

★ ★ ★ ★ ★

CONTENTS

THE
UNFINISHED HOUSE

CHAPTER I

A TELEPHONE CALL

"There's nothing exciting about real estate."

There was disappointment in Judy Bolton's voice. She had thought when Peter Dobbs established his new law office in Roulsville that there would be thrilling mystery cases for him to solve. But so far he had done nothing but draw up deeds, search titles and arrange first and second mortgages. It all seemed dreadfully dry and unexciting. All that rainy April afternoon as she and his sister Honey sat talking with him in the living room of Dr. Bolton's home, they had been trying to switch the conversation to the garden party. But just when they finally managed it the telephone rang. Judy went to answer it.

"It's Dad," she said, turning away from the

1

telephone. "He's calling from the hospital and he wants you, Peter. I can't think what for."

"Tell him I'm on my way."

And before Judy had time to question him, Peter was gone. She turned to Honey in complete surprise.

"Whatever possessed him?" she asked. "He acted as if it was urgent and yet I'm sure it isn't. Nobody we know is sick."

"It's probably only something about the garden party," Honey reassured her. "Peter is on the entertainment committee."

The garden party was to be a benefit for the hospital and every girl in Farringdon was looking forward to it. There had been a flurry of excited shopping for hats and garden party dresses. But Judy felt sure her hat was the loveliest of all. It dipped forward in a graceful curve above her forehead and was large and yellow and floppy with one enormous daisy fastened to the crown. She had a yellow dress to go with it and the dress flared out, making her look like a piece of sunshine. Judy's hair didn't seem quite so red when she was wearing yellow. She liked to think it even looked a little golden. But not beside Honey's. Peter's sister had hair the color of strained honey and a peaches-and-cream complexion that was beautiful under any hat. She was home from art school for the Easter vacation and had brought little dark-eyed Sylvia Weiss from New York with her. Sylvia had a table and was going to cut silhouettes.

If Judy hadn't been so interested in her clothes she might have felt a little left out of the program. So far, the entertainment committee had given her nothing to do.

"But I'll look sweet," she said, trying on her hat for the dozenth time and posing before the mirror. "Peter's so used to seeing me racing here and there after clues and getting into one jam after another solving mysteries that he ought to be happy to see me simply looking sweet."

"Peter isn't Arthur," Honey reminded her.

Judy laughed. Until just recently Arthur Farringdon-Pett, a young engineer with considerable influence in the town of Farringdon, had given a great deal of attention to her. But now he was engaged to Lorraine Lee, his own and his sister's friend since childhood.

"You mean I don't need to dress up for Peter? Nonsense! Any boy likes to see a girl dressed up. Maybe he'll let me sell flowers."

"And dwarf the poor things beside that daisy? No, darling," Honey objected, "let Lois and Lorraine peddle flowers on their own lawn. The garden party is on the Farringdon-Pett estate, you know, and Arthur will want them to. Peter has something more exciting for you to do. I'm sure that's what that telephone call was about."

"I'm pretty sure of it myself," Judy admitted. "But not quite. I wonder . . . " She plopped herself down in a low cushioned chair and looked thoughtful. Judy's favorite pastime was wondering. Lately Peter had been calling her the "I wonder girl."

Honey sighed. "Poor Judy! Nothing else to wonder about and so you bother your head over a simple telephone call."

"But Peter did act mysterious."

"It's a habit he has," Honey said. "He probably got it from going places with you."

"Probably," Judy agreed. "Horace has the same habit, being my brother. I think I hear him now. He'll have a copy of the paper with our garden party ad in it."

"The gate still creaks," Honey remarked as they heard it swing shut. Presently Judy's brother was standing in the doorway with his paper, Farringdon's one daily and the young reporter's joy and pride.

"There's your ad," he said, spreading the *Herald* out on the table. "Isn't it a beauty?"

Judy ran her finger down the list of attractions. Twelve booths with something interesting for sale in every one. A puppet show for the children. Iife-like silhouettes. Your photograph while you wait. Music. Entertainment. Prize limericks sung. Ice cream, cake, sandwiches and tea or lemonade for sale on the lawn. Flowers for sale.

"My what a lot of ways to spend money!"

"And it all goes to the hospital," Judy said. "Now Dad will be able to help his charity patients with free hospitalization. Really, it's wonderful. And we're just as glad to spend the money as the doctors and the hospital staff are to have it spent. Only Horace, what is this last attraction?"

The notice read: WIN-A-LOTTO. Big game with big prizes. Win a lot in an up-and-coming community. Roulsville Development Company.

"Oh, that's something new," Horace replied carelessly. "Fun for everybody. You play it a little like Bingo and a little like Lotto and a little like Tit Tat Toe. It's ten cents to try it."

"We can all play it then!" Honey cried. But Judy was skeptical.

"What is this Roulsville Development Company?" she asked. "Is it a firm of real estate men or just plain swindlers?"

"You can hardly swindle people by giving them things," Horace replied. "Anyway, it's the company Arthur's working for and I'm sure they're on the level."

"But it isn't the same company," Judy protested. "Arthur's drawing up plans for the Ace Builders and they have a contract with Roulsville Real Estate. Peter's been talking my ear off about it and so I know. They're two separate companies and neither of them have anything to do with this Roulsville Development Company."

"Holy Cats! Then I have put my foot in it!" Horace exclaimed. "I thought they were the same company and I was helping Arthur."

Judy gave a long sigh. "Well, you see now that you were helping his competitors."

"But if you win a lot," Horace argued, "it's yours and you can hire any builder you like—even the Ace Builders. The man said the lots were free and clear."

"What man was that?"

"A man," Horace said. "I didn't ask his name. He came into the *Herald* office and asked to see me. He explained that he wanted to raffle off lots at the garden party. It's just like any other raffle and all the money goes to the hospital. They're giving away a great many things like that at ten cents a chance."

"Yes, I know," Judy replied. "Home made quilts and embroidered bedspreads. Things like that. Not lots. This man . . . May I call him Mr. X, since you don't remember his name?"

Horace grinned. "Call him what you like."

"Well, this Mr. X," Judy went on, "couldn't possibly give away more than one lot at ten cents a chance and so the odds would be a hundred to one against any of us winning it. And if it's more than one lot . . . Honey," she interrupted herself, "wasn't Peter saying something about some free lot scheme he'd heard of? The lots were swampy or under water or something. Anyway, you couldn't build on them."

"These lots aren't like that," Horace protested. "They're all improved. Shade trees. Sewers. Everything. The man showed me a picture of them. In fact, he gave me a picture. We're running it along with a feature article about Roulsville in next Sunday's *Herald*. I've got a swell caption for it too, THE RESURRECTION OF THE GHOST TOWN.''

Honey shivered. "Ooo! That sounds spooky. People will love that."

But Judy was unimpressed. "I suppose Mr. X suggested the article?"

"He didn't exactly suggest it," Horace defended himself. "He merely mentioned the fact that the paper might give Roulsville a little boost."

"More free advertising for the Roulsville Development Company," Judy said dryly.

"You wouldn't feel that way about it if we won a lot."

"Indeed she wouldn't," Honey put in eagerly. "Judy was just saying there was nothing interesting about real estate. But here's something interesting. We might win a lot and move back to Roulsville just the way Grandpa and Grandma have always wanted to. Peter would like that. He says there's plenty for a lawyer to do in Roulsville. Most people are unfamiliar with building contracts and want legal advice before they buy property or build houses. But if we were to win a lot——''

"We might want legal advice more than ever," Judy put in hastily. "You should know, Honey, that people don't give things away without a reason. It looks to me as though somebody is trying to make a racket out of our hospital bazaar and I don't like it."

"Aw, Judy," Horace protested. "You've solved so many mysteries that you're just naturally suspicious of everybody."

"Even my own brother," she added pointedly. "You can bet your life I'm suspicious. I intend to find out just what this Roulsville Development Company is up to. And I'm going to do it before your Sunday feature article appears in the *Herald* and spoils all Arthur's plans for Roulsville Real Estate——''

"I told him his Utopian dream of a model town was a little too ambitions," Horace began pompously.

But Judy silenced him with a look. Horace certainly did have a talent for gumming things up. Here he had allowed Arthur's competitors to put on a show at the garden party and even advertised it in the paper. And all the time Judy had thought they were working together to plan a new and better town.

The old town was now only a memory. "And memories," Judy often thought as she recalled the terrors of the Roulsville disaster, "are the only true ghosts there are." Other ghost stories could be exploded. The story of the Roulsville flood could not.

Horace, too, would always recall it with a shudder. What other people called his heroism and what he still insisted was a miracle had saved the lives of the people. But their houses had been swept away.

Before the dam broke Grandpa and Grandma Dobbs had owned a beautiful corner house and Dr. Bolton had a fine home and a fine practice in Roulsville. But after the flood both families had been glad to sell their land and the wreckage of their homes and start over again in the nearby town of Farringdon. Now Arthur's company was buying up the property and building a model town out of the "ghost town" that had haunted the valley with its spectre-like broken dam ever since the disaster. Arthur had been engaged to lay out new streets, divide the land into generous-sized lots and design new houses to be constructed on them. Since Arthur was Judy's friend, she and Peter and Horace and Honey as well as Lois and Lorraine had had a great deal to say about it. They had even helped name the streets. There was a Lorraine Avenue and a Judy Lane and a Grace Court (for Honey's real name was Grace) and a Farringdon Boulevard which was big enough for Lois and Arthur both. Peter and Horace thought their names weren't suitable for streets—"hardly suitable for boys" they had explained jokingly. But Peter wasn't entirely practical about it. He declared his law office, when he had more than desk space in somebody else's building, would be situated on Judy Lane.

"It's terribly out-of-the-way."

But Judy's argument had left Peter undaunted. Judy Lane was in the very center of the new real estate development.

"I should think Arthur would be more interested in real estate than Peter," Judy said. "It's his business. He should have known about this before. I think I'll call him up."

Their conversation was brief. Judy sighed as she hung up the receiver.

"Oh, well!" she said. "It wouldn't have mattered. Arthur says his company couldn't afford to buy up all the land and this Roulsville Development Company has just as much right to improve the town as they have. I wish now I'd listened a little more carefully to what Peter was telling me. He'd know whether or not it's legal to raffle off lots at a party.''

There really was no use getting stirred up about it, Judy decided. Arthur didn't need her to solve his problems. He had Lorraine. But just the same, something Peter had said when she was listening kept recurring to her.

''It isn't Public Enemy Number One I'm going after. Let the big lawyers take care of him and his kind. I'm out to get the slick criminals who think they have the law behind them. Criminals in business. It may not sound as exciting as a murder mystery. But it's a darned sight more important. A murderer kills only one man but these real estate sharpers can ruin a whole town full. That's why there's a place for me in Roulsville.''

Dear Peter! He'd never failed anyone. He'd win his reputation, not by spectacular defenses of gangsters and murderers, but by his honesty and courage in protecting the little man.

A place for Peter in Roulsville?

''Yes,'' Judy thought, ''and if I can help him, there may be a place for me.''

CHAPTER II

"STILL the 'I wonder' girl," Peter said jokingly when Judy asked him about the telephone call he had received. She had meant to ask him about the raffle too. There was a great deal she had meant to ask him. But he was hurrying off somewhere and she didn't see him again until the day of the garden party. By that time she had forgotten everything else in the pleasure of appearing on the spacious Farringdon-Pett lawns in her beautiful new hat.

Peter hadn't given much time to the entertainment committee, although he was supposed to be on it, and so Horace found a booth for his sister. Judy, in her yellow outfit, was to be at the pet shop. Honey had said that, selling flowers, her daisy would dwarf the other flowers. Now, selling baby chicks, she thought the flower might dwarf them too. But people like tiny chicks. It was just after Easter and many of the children who came to the garden

13

party still had their Easter baskets and thought a baby chick would make them complete.

"I got a whole basketful of eggs," one sweet-faced little blonde boy confided in Judy, "but somebody'd boiled them all so they didn't hatch a single baby chick."

"Did you expect they would?" Judy laughed.

" 'Course I did. Eggs are s'posed to hatch, aren't they? Isn't that where chickens come from—out of eggs?"

Judy looked at the little boy's mother and their eyes met in a twinkle of understanding. She was a young, pretty woman. But tired-looking, Judy thought. Her eyes, in spite of their twinkle, held some sadness just below the surface. Dark pools, they were, with star shine reflected on the top. Judy felt she'd like to know this woman, to talk with her, to make things a little easier for her. Her shoulders stooped as though they had carried some too-heavy burden.

"We'll buy you a chick," she said to the little boy. "Maybe we'll win a lot to go with it. The chicken ought to have some place to scratch."

But her "Maybe we'll win a lot" sounded a little wistful. Judy's heart went out in sympathy. It didn't matter any more whether or not she won a lot. She wanted this stranger to win if that would take the shadows out of her eyes and the stoop from her shoulders. Life shouldn't do things like that to people unless it turned about and gave them some happiness besides. But would a free lot bring happiness with it? The crowds of people Judy heard talking all seemed to think that it would.

"They're literally giving the town away," Judy heard somebody remark. "It's a chance that comes once in a life time."

"That's the way I ought to feel," Judy told herself. "It's dreadfully annoying to be so suspicious of things. Now if I were anybody but myself or if I'd had a chance to ask Peter . . . "

She looked all around the grounds. The little boy and his mother were walking across the lawn with their downy purchase in a cardboard box punched with holes. The chicken was peeping and the boy was chattering and the woman with the far-away, sad look in her eyes was laughing as though it had been a long time since she had laughed about anything. Many of the people on the lawn were Judy's friends and many whom she did not know knew her either through newspaper publicity or because of her father's practice. Lois and Lorraine, Connie Gray, Betty, Marge and Tagalong with her new chum, Selma Brady, all were there. Sylvia Weiss sat demurely at her silhouette table cutting out the profiles of people from a sheet of black paper. The boys were there too—Arthur, tall and distinguished-looking; Horace chattering away like a magpie with some of his newspaper friends. But where was Peter? He'd said he'd be at the garden party early. It was too late for that already.

"He'll be here pretty soon," Honey kept reassuring her as the minutes ticked away.

Judy couldn't help looking at her watch every minute or so. The garden party wouldn't be half as much fun without Peter. He wouldn't even see her in her lovely hat.

A puppet show was next on the program. Children shoved forward to where the operator of the show was already pushing his funny little dolls up from behind the velvet curtain. Punch was quarreling with Judy in his squeaky, mechanical voice and all the children were laughing and rocking back and forth on the grass.

It was *Peter* and Judy that ought to be talking. She felt more and more certain that she ought to ask him about the lots that were going to be given away. The announcer said "lots". Everybody said "lots". But if they gave away more than one lot at ten cents a chance . . . well, Judy simply couldn't see how an honest company could afford it.

The puppet show ended at last when a huge alligator came up from behind the curtain and swallowed Punch. The next attraction was the limerick singer.

"I'm going to try for this one," Selma Brady stopped to whisper in Judy's ear.

"You ought to be good at it. Remember how we made up a play in verse?"

"Of course I remember. But Judy, you ought to be good at it too. There's a prize for the best limerick and this fellow, Al Allison, sings it to the tune of his piano accordian."

"Oh, good!" Judy cried. "I love accordian music. The last time I heard it was at Scottie's housewarming."

"Scottie's here somewhere. That's what I came over to tell you. She said she'd relieve you at your booth any time you wanted her."

"That's sweet of her. But it was really Peter I wanted. I'm a little suspicious of this real estate company and their game and I wanted to ask him about it. But I don't see him anywhere.''

''I don't either. But why are you suspicious, Judy?''

She laughed. ''What a question! It's just my nature, I guess. You helped me solve a mystery once. You ought to know that.''

''You see mysteries in lots of ordinary things, Judy.''

''Do I? And real estate is awfully ordinary. I told Peter so only last week. But I'm beginning to change my mind.''

''Maybe we can think up a limerick about real estate,'' Selma suggested eagerly. ''It ought to go well with the game:

''There was a young man in our town
Who thought real estate values were down
        But they mounted sky high
        When he started to buy . . . ''

She thought a minute. ''Now I am stuck. You'll have to help me out, Judy. What rhymes with town?''

''Oh, frown . . . drown . . . crown . . . ''

There was a crowd around them now, all making suggestions. Lois, Lorraine and

Honey each had a word to offer. But nothing
seemed to fit properly into the last line.

Judy tried changing the verse around:

"There was a young fellow in brown
Who said real estate values were down.
    But we know they are high
    And we all wonder why
He's giving away half the town."

"Why, that's splendid!" Selma praised her.

"Your verse inspired it," Judy said as she
finished in a howl of applause. "It's true too.
Horace's mysterious Mr. X was wearing a
brown suit and they are going to raffle off *lots*
—not just one lot. And so it could easily be
half the town."

"Who is Mr. X?" Lorraine asked curiously.

"That's what I'd like to know," Judy answered. "Horace doesn't remember anything
about him except that he was wearing a brown
suit and that he had a moustache. He didn't
find out his name and yet he gave him permission to conduct this game and promised to run
a feature article about Roulsville. He hasn't
run the article yet."

"When I do," Horace said, "it's going to
be good."

"But I still don't see why you call the man Mr. X," Lorraine persisted.

"Because," Judy said with a flourish of the hot dog on roll that she had forgotten to eat, "X stands for the unknown and this man is the *unknownest*——"

"There's no superlative to unknown," Horace interrupted.

Honey interrupted too—with a giggle. "Don't be a dictionary, Horace. We're having a good time."

"He's not being a dictionary," Lois put in. "He's being an English grammar."

"An English grandmother, did you say?"

But Lois' answer was lost in a scream of laughter. Judy choked on her hot dog. But, out of sympathy for Horace, she sent him to turn in her limerick and re-establish his dignity. She saw him hand it to Al Allison and then she saw the limerick singer hand it back to another, shorter man with a florid face and a rim of thin hair around the edge of his egg-shaped bald head. The bald-headed man scowled and put the verse in his pocket. But Al Allison didn't sing it. Judy and her friends listened, hoping he would. He sang a great many that weren't half as well written. He could make verses that didn't even rhyme sound as though they were good by adding his own catchy chorus. His voice was enchanting. It had a quality to it that made more than one person ask, "Who is he?" when the act was over.

But nobody seemed to know. Several people said his voice sounded familiar and Judy thought so too but nobody could connect it with anything definite. Sylvia Weiss was quite positive she had heard it in New York and Lois and Lorraine were equally positive they had heard it some time ago in Farringdon. Horace said the limerick singer was not the gentleman Judy referred to as "the mysterious Mr. X."

"But he's every bit as mysterious," he added. "With a voice like that he ought to be known all over the country."

"Maybe he is," Judy said, "and it's just because we Farringdonites are dumb that we don't recognize him."

"Or maybe because he's dumb that he didn't recognize your verse," Selma Brady put in. "It was really good."

"It wasn't bad anyway," Judy admitted. "I don't think he objected to the verse *as a verse*. It was something I said in it. I bet you he's connected with this real estate firm himself and I said something a little too true. I wonder what it was.''

Judy went back to her booth still wondering. Scottie, who had been taking care of the pets in her absence, turned to her with a smile.

"Business was good," she said. "I sold five canary birds and three puppies and I don't know how many baby chicks."

"You sold that spotted pup," Judy observed, looking into the puppy pen. "I'm glad. He annoyed the others by whining. Now if we can only get rid of the biggest parrot——"

"He is a nuisance," Scottie agreed, "saying 'shut up' to all the customers. It's awfully rude of him. But you can't expect parrots to have manners."

"Hardly," laughed Judy as she took her place in the booth and looked over the crowd, still hoping to spot Peter. Scottie looked too.

"There goes your hat," she said as she discovered another girl with a hat like Judy's.

Judy flushed pink. "It doesn't matter anyway. Peter isn't here to see it."

But after Scottie had left the booth, the parrot kept croaking, "There goes your hat!"

"I'd like to wring your neck," Judy said.

"I'd like to wring your neck," the parrot repeated to Judy's next lady customer. And when the game of Win-a-Lotto was announced, it actually called out, "Razzberries!"

It was then that the limerick singer offered to buy it. "Clever bird, might teach it a few limericks." He turned to Judy and said, "You should have tried for a limerick yourself."

It was on the tip of Judy's tongue to say, "I did try." But she caught herself in time. If this man had anything to do with the real estate business it might be just as well if he didn't recognize Judy as the author of the objectionable verse.

"I'm saving my wits for the game," she said. "I'd love to win a lot in Roulsville. I used to live there before the flood and I've always hoped I might move back some day. It's really my home."

"So you'd like to win a lot?"

"Indeed I would," she replied evenly. "But so would a great many other people. There's a woman with a little boy here and she has her heart set on winning. Do you think she has a chance?"

"Her chance is as good as anybody's. Maybe better," he added as he turned to go. "Play your hardest, everybody!" he called out. "The game's beginning now!"

The girl with a hat like Judy's passed by her booth again just as the limerick singer began passing out cards with numbers printed on them. Judy looked at the girl. Yes, the hats were as like as two peas. It was annoying when Judy had chosen hers so carefully. Dear! Dear! If it could only have been a nice girl wearing her hat. But this girl had a hard face and a "try and put anything over on me" air that made Judy wonder if she might not be putting something over on somebody else. She was sure of it a moment later when she crossed the lawn for a glass of lemonade and a man stopped her and whispered in her ear, "Watch out for suckers."

"I will," she whispered back. But she didn't let him see her face and, consequently, she could not see his. "He thinks I'm the other girl in the yellow hat," she thought. But she was no longer annoyed because the stranger had a hat like hers. "Suckers? So she's looking for suckers, is she? And this is a racket. Thank you, hat," she said softly, "for giving me another mystery to solve."

CHAPTER III

Now that Judy had proof that Win-a-Lotto was something more than a raffle, she was determined to find Peter. She asked everybody if they had seen him but nobody had. At least, nobody was very positive about it. Two or three people said they had seen him with Judy but Judy herself knew that was impossible. Where was he?

The question remained unanswered as did all the other questions Judy would have asked Peter if she had been able to find him. The only way to learn anything about the game now was to play it and see what happened. Numbers were printed on the Win-a-Lotto cards that had been handed out and people were supposed to match their numbers with the numbers being called by the announcer or rather, the limerick singer, for they were one and the same. The man's voice was musical even when he was not singing. Judy felt more sure than ever that she had heard it before.

The woman with the little boy who had bought the chicken was standing next to Judy, eagerly checking off numbers on her card. She had already signed her name and address on the card in the space provided for it and now, like everybody else, she was trying to get three numbers in a row. That was the object of the game.

"It looks so easy," she sighed. "If only I win!"

"I'd like to win too," Judy confided, "if only to find out what happens. I wanted to ask a friend of mine about it but he's not here and it's nearly four——"

"Nearly four! Good gracious!" the woman exclaimed. "I'll have to go then. Will you girls keep an eye on Algernon and, if it isn't too much trouble, I wish you'd check off the numbers on my card."

"We'd be glad to," Judy agreed, taking the card. She had been hoping for a chance to make friends with the woman and it was almost as easy to check off two sets of numbers as one. She glanced at the boy whose lip was beginning to tremble as he watched his mother cross the grass and disappear through the gate. What a little fellow he was to have a big name like

Algernon! She had heard his mother call him Algie and decided to do the same.

"Here, Algie," she said, "maybe you'd like to do this for your mother. You know these numbers, don't you?"

"Sure I know 'em. But when is Mommie coming back?"

"Oh, pretty soon. She wouldn't leave you alone for very long. Besides, we're looking after you."

"Like I'm looking after my chicken," the boy agreed, "that is, 'til we win him a lot. Gee! Won't it be swell to have a whole lot?" He lifted his face, all traces of tears gone. "It's nice to be looked after," he said. "Mommie leaves me lots of time—with nobody."

"But now you have your chicken."

"For comp'ny—when Mommie goes away. Where do you s'pose she went?"

"I don't know. But she'll be back. Look here, Algie. You missed a number."

Judy showed him where to mark it down and he rested the card on top of his chicken box and followed the announcer's voice eagerly with his pencil. In a surprisingly short time Judy and the little boy both had three numbers in a row and went to hand in their cards.

"But we couldn't both win," Algie was saying anxiously and Judy was thinking the same thing. Only her thoughts went further. "At least, if I win, I'll have a chance to investigate this thing. I won't be one of the suckers I was supposed to watch for."

The limerick singer was collecting the cards and tearing them in half.

"Save your check," he was saying in that still-familiar musical voice of his, "it may mean you are a winner."

Judy noticed he had a handful of cards already.

"I guess we all got three in a row," Honey said, running up with her card at the same time. "I did and so did Lois and Lorraine and Selma Brady and Sylvia Weiss and a lot of others. You were right, Judy, about him giving away half the town."

"*If* he's giving it away. Didn't you hear him say, 'It may mean you are a winner'? That sounds as if there's more to this little game than we know. If the lots really aren't free one little boy is going to be dreadfully disappointed."

"Who is he?" Honey asked.

"Believe it or not," Judy replied, "his name

is Algernon. But his mother calls him Algie
—Algie Piper. I was talking with her before
and she introduced herself as Mrs. Piper. She
seemed awfully anxious to win a lot. Her husband is going to work in the new Roulsville
paper mill and they'll have to buy or rent a
house in the town anyway. But I'm more sure
by the minute that this game is a swindle.''

''What did Peter say about it?'' Honey
asked.

''Why, Honey!'' Judy exclaimed. ''I
thought you knew I couldn't find him.''

''But I saw you talking with him just a
moment ago.''

''He's here then?''

''He was here. Didn't you say anything to
him about it?''

''But I didn't see him,'' Judy protested.
''You couldn't have seen me talking with him.''

''I know it was Peter,'' Honey maintained,
''and it must have been you. There isn't anybody else here with a hat like yours.''

''Oh, yes there is! But I didn't know Peter
knew her,'' Judy added in bewilderment.
''It's funny he'd come here and not even stop
at my booth. Has something happened that
you haven't told me?''

"Why, no——"

Now Honey was bewildered too. The two girls stood looking at each other, forgetting the garden party and its long list of attractions in this new problem that had confronted them.

"Could it be a law suit?" Judy asked at last.

"Peter would have told us at dinner table. He always does."

"Then maybe it's just the girl—or the hat. Peter didn't even see me in my hat like it. And you say he's not attracted by clothes!"

"There's certainly something funny about it," Honey agreed. "But let's forget it. It can't do any good to worry. When's this little boy's mother coming back? I wanted you to go with me and have our pictures taken or our fortunes told or something."

Judy laughed. "I'm not interested in pictures and you know how I feel about fortunes. I'm sure Algie's better off just staying here by the pet booth where his mother will be sure to find him."

"I'll get us all some ice cream then," Honey suggested.

Presently she returned with three large cones and the news that Peter and the girl with the hat like Judy's weren't on the grounds any more. She had guessed Algie's choice of ice cream. Strawberry. He grinned over the cone.

"I didn't have any before," he said. "I spent my dime for the baby chick and Mommie spent hers for the lot. We only had two dimes."

"Your mother probably has plenty more in her pocketbook," laughed Judy. "How do you suppose she buys the food you eat?"

"She charges it," the little boy replied promptly.

"That's one way of doing it."

"But the milk man wouldn't let her have the milk this morning," Algie went on sorrowfully, "so I drank tea and it's nasty without milk."

"Tea's not good for little boys."

"That's what my mommie says," Algie agreed. "But she says it's better than nothing and Daddy's going to send home some money next week. He's staying with my grandma but now I'bet he'll come home 'cause I won a lot and we're going to move into a beautiful new house——"

"Algie, dear," Judy said gently. "There isn't any house on the lot yet. It's just a piece of land."

"Then we'll build a house."

"It takes money to build a house and maybe you'll find the numbers you had weren't lucky numbers and they didn't win after all."

"B-but they've got to."

"I know how you feel," Judy sympathized. "But lots of times people have to go without things they want. Sometimes they go without things they really need. And sometimes," Judy added more cheerfully, "it makes them brave and strong to go without things. Abraham Lincoln didn't have very much, you know."

"He had a house, even if it was logs. Maybe we could build a log house on our lot. I think I could cut down trees if somebody gave me an axe."

There was no curbing his enthusiasm. He kept on talking like that, suggesting log houses and stone houses and even a tent like Indians. And, while he was talking, Judy was fast selling out her stock of pets. It was growing late and people were leaving the garden party. They went in groups, chatting as they went. Judy heard the word "lot" mentioned several times as the laughing groups of people passed by her booth. Still Algie's mother did not come.

"She knew who you were," Honey suggested.

"If you went home and took the little boy with you, she'd know where to find him."

"Want to come home with me?" Judy asked of the tired little fellow. "I'll show you lots of interesting things. I have a secret drawer in my dresser and there's an attic in our house with a funny little ladder up to it and a hollow tree in front where a little squirrel lives. Maybe you won't see the squirrel. But I have a lovely big black cat that you will see."

"He'll eat my chicken," Algie protested, pulling his hand away from Judy's and backing into one corner of the booth. The chicken, in its cardboard box, was held tightly in his hand and was beginning its sleepy good-night trill.

"Blackberry's a good cat," Judy reassured him. "He doesn't catch birds and so I'm sure he wouldn't hurt your chicken."

"I don't like cats," the little boy wailed. "And I want my mommie!"

"We'll put the cat out then," Judy said cheerfully. "I have a mommie too and I'm sure you'll like her. She'll cook you a nice dinner. And I have a nice daddy too. He has a cupboard full of toys for his little patients to play with. He's a doctor."

Algie turned terrified eyes to Judy.

"Your d-daddy's a d-doctor?"

She nodded.

"Then he takes little boys off to the hospital just like p'licemen take them off to jail. No!" he screamed. "I won't go! The doctor will stick needles in me and the cat will eat my chicken and I w-want my MOM-MIE!"

This last was a shrill wail. Algie kept it up, beating his fists on the counter and kicking the underneath part of the booth with his feet until what few pets Judy had left huddled off to the corners of their pens in terror.

"I won't have needles in me! I want my mommie! Where is my mom-mie?" echoed over the whole garden.

And now the chief attraction at the garden party was little Algernon Piper with his chicken and his half of the Win-a-Lotto ticket and his shrill, terrified wail.

CHAPTER IV

JUST as little Algie Piper opened his mouth to let out a louder wail than any he had yet uttered, Peter Dobbs arrived. He sauntered in through the gate exactly as though he were arriving at two o'clock, as he had promised, instead of six.

Algie's wails reached his ears and a broad grin spread over his face as he hurried to the pet booth.

"Just in time to help you out of a situation," he began good-naturedly.

Judy looked up when she heard his voice. What was he grinning about? The meanie! Disappointing her like that and then laughing over her predicament.

"Just *too late* to help me out, you'd better say," she retorted. "If you'd been here as you promised you might have helped a lot of people. But I suppose that girl was more important——"

Peter looked dumbfounded.

"More important than this party? Why, heck! Of course she was."

That wasn't at all what Judy had expected. She had expected an apology. Peter's reply left her speechless.

"You see, I couldn't wait. You do see that, don't you, Judy? Miss Ames called for me this afternoon——"

"So it's Miss Ames?" Judy asked icily. "I've been wondering who she was. I suppose you mistook her for me in that hat and just naturally walked off with her."

"Be reasonable," Peter said. "The boy's making scene enough without our quarreling in public."

"All right," Judy agreed, "we'll wait and quarrel in private after I've taken this yelling kid home."

"I'm not a yelling kid!" Algie screamed. "And I can go home ALO-ONE!"

"All right. Go alone. And I'll follow you to see that you get there safely. How about your supper?" Judy asked. "Suppose we stop at the store and buy a box of cereal and some crackers and milk just to make sure you don't go to bed hungry?"

"May I come along?" Peter asked meekly.

"Oh, I suppose so," Judy replied, "but if you wanted to come some place with me I can't see why you didn't come to the garden party as you promised. Everybody was expecting you. Arthur and Horace and Donald Carter and all the boys but you were helping. Honey thought you'd be here and naturally I expected you."

"Judy, please!"

"Please what?"

"Lay off. I've had about all I can take. Can't we just walk along peaceably and argue about this another time?"

With a sigh, Judy assented. She had no great desire for an argument herself. As tired as she was puzzled, she fell into step with Peter while Algie trudged ahead. Honey had already gone home as she knew she must help her grandmother. Old Mrs. Dobbs was growing very feeble and she depended on Honey. There was a woman who came in to cook and clean but Honey did the little, thoughtful things whenever she was home. When she wasn't, Peter did them. Judy might have remembered this at any other time but his arrival had been badly timed and when he mentioned Miss Ames—well, that was too much. Judy could forgive the girl for having a hat like hers and even for having a smirk on her face in place of a smile. But she could not forgive her for taking Peter away on the very afternoon when she had planned to look her prettiest and ask him things in which he was sure to be interested. She couldn't forgive Peter either. And now she didn't want to ask him anything.

They walked along in silence. Peter's occasional remarks were met with stony indifference and so he gave his attention to the little boy and they talked about the chicken. That was how, without Judy's saying a word, he learned of the free lot raffle and demanded an explanation.

"Miss Ames can explain *that* a great deal better than I can," Judy returned coldly. "I thought perhaps she was explaining it this afternoon. Or weren't you talking business?"

"Well, not exactly——"

"It might pay you to talk business then," Judy interrupted. "I thought you were going to be 'a friend of the little man'. Well, the little man in Roulsville may need a friend before very long but he's not going to hire a lawyer who's too close to these real estate racketeers. I'd advise you to drop your new flame before she burns your hand."

"I don't know what you're talking about,"
Peter replied. "Surely you don't mind my helping a poor little girl."

Judy sniffed. Miss Ames didn't impress her
as being either very poor or very little.

"I'd rather you didn't mention that girl
again," she said.

"Very well. I guess I figured you out all
wrong, Judy. I thought you'd understand."

Peter sighed and little Algie looked up at him,
imitating his sigh. Even Judy had to laugh at
that. Young Algernon, when he wasn't in a
tantrum, seemed a pleasant, intelligent little
fellow, quite capable of looking after himself.
He carried the house key in his pocket and let
himself into the bare kitchen without fear.

"I tell you, Mommie goes away lots of times
and leaves me alone. I'm not afraid here," he
explained. "I was just scared with a lot of
people at a party. An' when you said *doctor*—"
He lowered his voice to a whisper. He might
have been saying *kidnapper* or *cannibal*. "A
doctor," he repeated, "who sticks needles in
people and takes them off to the hospital to
be cut up——"

"Oh, Algie!"

"But doctors do cut people up."

"They make people well," Judy said, "and when they operate——"

"That's cutting people up!"

". . . they only do it to save people's lives and make them well and strong," Judy finished, disregarding the interruption. She turned to Peter and said in a lower voice, "That's the sort of thing my father has to contend with—parents who plant fear in their children's hearts and then act surprised when they refuse to take their medicine or be examined by a doctor."

Peter smiled. Judy was being herself again.

"We'll overcome that," he said. "We can do a great many things—together."

His honest blue eyes looked down at Judy and he had her hand, there in the bare little kitchen with the boy beside them. For a moment she forgot everything but the fact that Peter was there and they were safe and soon there would be a fire and a bubbling pot of coffee and warm cereal for Algie. For they had decided to keep him company since they were hungry themselves and since his mother, wherever she went, would probably welcome a cup of coffee when she returned.

Judy set the table with cracked bowls and a handleless cup for herself. It was habit that made her place the one good cup for Peter. Algie drank his milk out of a tin mug with Humpty Dumpty imprinted in the tin.

"Gee! This milk tastes good." He smacked his lips as he lifted the cup to take another swallow. Then, suddenly, he put the cup down. "Better save this," he told himself manfully. "It'll taste good for breakfast."

"Go ahead! Drink it. There's plenty more for breakfast. I'll put it here in the pantry window," Judy said. "It ought to keep."

She returned with a glass of calvesfoot jelly. She held it up.

"Look what I found! Here, Algie! How'd you like a little jelly with your cracker?"

"That's not jelly," he said, making a face. "That's medicine. Mommie said so. She said I wasn't to touch it."

"Very well." Judy sat down the glass. There wasn't much she could do about it if "Mommie said so". But what was the boy's mother thinking of—leaving him alone so much, making him afraid of doctors and calling the one bit of good food in the house "medicine" so he would not touch it? And she had seemed such a nice woman too. Judy could not understand it.

It was late when Mrs. Piper finally came home. Judy and Peter had managed to get Algie into his pajamas and he was just dozing off to sleep when she opened the door. Up he popped, like a jack-in-the-box, wide awake and wanting to know where she had been.

"Now darling," the woman said firmly, "I told you that now you are a big boy you must let Mommie go where she likes. I let you go and don't ask questions."

"If it was a movie," Algie said, "I want to hear the story."

"Then go to sleep like a good boy and I'll tell you the story in the morning."

Judy and Peter exchanged one bewildered glance before Mrs. Piper turned to them and thanked them for staying with Algie. "But it wasn't necessary," she added, "he could have managed for himself."

Judy hardly saw how, with nothing to eat in the house but a jar of calvesfoot jelly which he had been told was medicine. Then she remembered the crackers and was surprised to see how hungrily Mrs. Piper ate them. She drank the coffee in grateful gulps. Poor woman! She had needed the coffee. As Judy and Peter watched her, neither of them could believe she really had been to a movie. She was in some trouble, Judy felt sure. And if winning a lot meant more trouble . . . But it mustn't! She told her about the Win-a-Lotto ticket and at the same time warned her not to trust the Roulsville Development Company.

"They are probably only trying to trick people with their free lot story," she said. "I tried to tell Algie but he's dead sure he's going to have a big lot with a place for the chicken to scratch and a beautiful house for himself."

"Poor Algie!" his mother said. "His chicken will be luckier than we are if it gets enough to eat, let alone a place to scratch."

"You're not really counting on winning a lot then?"

"I was," Mrs. Piper said sadly. "I didn't think of it being crooked and I thought we might get some loan company to advance the money to build a house. This shack may be worth something for the land it's on and there are such things as mortgages, though I don't understand them. My husband's job will be steady and I'm sure he'll be well enough to work soon. He's getting well now—at his mothers where he can be quiet and not worry and where Algie's screaming won't unsettle his nerves again. He's had—a breakdown. He doesn't know how badly things have been going. I haven't told him. He sends what money he thinks we'll need. But it isn't enough.''

"I see," Judy said softly.

"And now," the woman continued, "if I should win a lot and if I should be able to have a clean, comfortable home waiting for him and if—if—" Her voice trembled and her eyes filled, suddenly, with tears. "So many ifs! I sometimes wonder what's the use of trying. I sometimes think I'd like to let go and have a breakdown too.''

"But you mustn't," Judy chided her gently. "A family needs at least one strong person in it and you have to be that one.''

"I guess I do," she admitted. "You understand a lot for such a young girl.''

"Not half as much as I'd like to understand," Judy said. "I'm so reckless sometimes. Peter knows, don't you, Peter?''

He nodded, grinning a little.

"Reckless, yes. But understanding just the same—at least you were.''

Now why did he have to add that, Judy wondered. She wanted to forget their quarrel but she could no more forget it than she could forget

Mrs. Piper's sad eyes or the little boy's frightened, bewildered wail. So many things wrong in the world and so few strong people to set them right!

"I must be one of the strong ones," Judy told herself as she and Peter walked out into the dimly lighted street.

She tried to see his face, glad that the darkness covered hers for hot tears were beginning to trickle down her cheeks. In spite of her resolution, she did not feel strong tonight. She and Peter had done so many things together that she had begun to count on him always to help her. She had never thought of another girl stepping in and taking her place. Now another girl had stepped in. Would it mean that she must solve this new mystery alone?

CHAPTER V

It was Honey who told Peter what she knew of the game, Win-a-Lotto. Judy was too hurt to tell him anything. But she did listen to Honey. Peter's sister was puzzled too.

"He acted real mad about it when I told him," she said. "He blamed you, Judy. He blamed you even more than he did Horace because he said if you'd listened to him the other day when he was explaining this racket you'd have known right off that it wasn't honest and you'd have stopped it even if you weren't on the entertainment committee."

"But how unfair," Judy said, "to blame me when I tried my very best to get in touch with him and ask him——"

"Perhaps he didn't know that."

"He certainly did. That day Dad called him to the hospital—I never did know what for—I called up and asked to speak with him. The girl at the switchboard told me he was still there an she'd have him call me. But he didn't call. And they don't forget to give messages at the hospital.''

''It is queer,'' Honey admitted, ''but Judy, there's a lot we don't know yet. If you'd only have faith in Peter——''

''Faith!'' Judy scoffed. ''I never did see much sense in having faith without reason. I've often thought I'd like to add to that saying about Faith, Hope and Charity, 'and the least of these is Faith' .''

But Honey was remembering a long way back. ''You've doubted Peter before—and you've always been wrong. And I remember how it hurt when you didn't have faith in me.''

Judy slid down in the hammock closer to Honey. The two girls were sitting in the hammock on the porch of Judy's home. Blackberry was purring and stretching his paws in the space between them and little checks of sunlight kissed their faces through the lattice work. Judy lifted Blackberry to her arms as she crowded him out of his place. He was too big to sit on her shoulder the way he used to when Peter first gave him to her. So he sprawled across her lap, purring louder than ever as he dozed back to sleep.

''Perhaps you're right,'' Judy admitted, ''and

I do need to have more faith in Peter. But Honey, suppose you look at the other side of the picture. You say I have too little faith. But isn't it true that most people have too much? All the innocent people who are swindled out of their land and their money have faith in the very people who are robbing them. Swindlers count on that. They look for trustful people— people who will believe the lies they tell. And then, behind their back, they call them suckers.''

''I guess Mrs. Piper is what they'd call a sucker then?''

''She gives that impression,'' Judy replied, ''but whether she is or not remains to be seen. Honey, isn't that Mrs. Piper coming up the walk now—with Algie?''

Honey looked, then nodded slowly.

''She seems excited about something,'' Judy went on. ''See how fast she's walking. And Algie's skipping and jumping up and down. Maybe they did win a lot. Oh, Honey! I almost hope—they didn't.''

Judy had lowered her voice for Mrs. Piper was coming up on the porch now. She hadn't seen the girls in the hammock. Blackberry jumped down, as he always did when people came, and walked sedately over to the door where he sat on the mat, his tail straight out behind him.

"Bad cat!" Algie said. "Get out the way, bad cat!" And he gave him a push with the toe of his shoe.

Blackberry was not used to this sort of treatment. Usually the children who came to Dr. Bolton's house were as gentle with him as he was with them. But the cat did not yowl. He merely looked up and said with his reproachful eyes, "Little boy, you have a lot to learn."

Mrs. Piper was about to ring the bell when Judy called from the hammock.

"Here we are! Or did you want to see Dad?"

Turning with a quick smile, Mrs. Piper discovered Judy and Honey in their cool retreat behind the lattices.

"How lovely!" she exclaimed. "Why, it's just like a living room here on the porch. Only there's sunshine and a little bit of shadow and a hammock to be lazy in. I've always wanted a hammock. Algie," she said, turning to the little boy with shining eyes, "we'll have a porch like this on our house—a wide porch with lattice work and a hammock."

"Gee, Mommie!" Algie said, "I wouldn't

mind taking naps in a hammock. Can we have a back yard with swings and slides in it and a play house for Clara's dolls?"

"Who's Clara?" Judy asked. "Not a little girl friend—so soon."

"Clara is his sister," Mrs. Piper explained with a queer look toward Algie. "She's away on a visit."

"To my aunts," Algie put in, "and she's been away all Spring just having a good time and Mommie won't let me go too."

"Hush, Algie! You mustn't talk like that," his mother chided him. "Mommie needs you here—her little man. You helped win the lot, you know. And you did too, Miss Bolton."

"Did I? Did you, I mean—win a lot?" Judy stammered. "I'm glad you told me."

"But you don't seem happy about it!"

"She's suspicious," Honey put in. "Sometimes it pays to be suspicious at first—until you see what you've won."

"We're going to see this afternoon. That's what we came about," Mrs. Piper explained. "We wanted you girls to go with us."

"We'll go gladly," Judy told her. "We weren't doing a thing. I suppose the real estate people are taking you in their car?"

"But there's plenty of room. They'll take you too."

"If they won't," Honey said, "we can come along afterwards in Peter's car."

Judy's lips tightened. "I'd rather ride with the salesman," she said firmly. "I don't need Peter to help solve this mystery."

So it was decided that Mrs. Piper should ask the real estate salesman to stop off at thirteen sixty-five Grove Street and collect Judy and Honey before he drove on to Roulsville. They were supposed to be ready at two o'clock and Judy promised that they would be waiting on the porch. But two o'clock came—and half past two—and no salesman stopped and there was no word at all from Mrs. Piper.

"Maybe there wasn't room enough in the car," Judy said, "but at least she could have telephoned. If there's anything that makes me boil it's having people break appointments. That's what I can't understand about Peter. He knew I was expecting him."

"And so did Mrs. Piper. Dear me!" Honey sighed. "Can't we depend on anybody?"

"We can depend on each other," Judy reminded her.

"Yes, and we can depend on Peter too, even

though it doesn't always seem so. You know in
your heart that we can.''

"I know things with my head," Judy answered, "not my heart."

"But Judy dear, you have to use them both,"
Honey said softly. "Even if Peter is having
a silly affair with a girl not worth bothering
about, some day he'll come back and want you
to forgive him."

"He needn't," Judy said. "I'm not the only
girl in the world and Peter isn't the only boy."

"Of course, dear, we don't have to plan things
now—though I would like you for a sister,"
Honey added, giving Judy's hand an affection-
ate squeeze.

"Silly! Girls don't usually marry in order
to have nice sisters-in-law though you might
think so to watch Lois and Lorraine. Honestly,
sometimes I think Arthur fell in love with Lorraine because Lois was so fond of her. But it's
a nice reason anyhow," Judy decided, "and I'm
glad Arthur and I can keep on being friends.
I'm more interested right now in his model town
than I am in Peter's legal affairs."

"Perhaps that's the whole trouble."

"I never thought," Judy said, "that you'd

be scolding me for anything. It used to be the other way around.''

"Indeed it did,'' laughed Honey. "But now you need scolding. You're just sitting here, Judy Bolton, and letting a mystery slip right through your fingers because Mrs. Piper broke her appointment and you're too stubborn to ask Peter to drive us to Roulsville.''

"I am not stubborn,'' Judy said. "I'm just angry and hurt——''

"And you won't give in,'' Honey finished, "and that's being stubborn and it won't get us to Roulsville.''

Judy had to admit Honey was right. It didn't get her anywhere simply to be stubborn. It would be far better to pretend everything between them was exactly as it had been before the garden party. No questions. No explanations. Yes, Judy decided, she would make herself forget the whole thing if it was, as Honey said, only a silly affair.

"Well, I suppose—'' Judy began. But Honey was already on her way to the telephone. Peter said he'd be right over and he was there almost as quickly as it took him to say so.

"You can tell me where we're going when

we're on our way,'' he laughed as the two girls climbed into the back seat of his little car. He had had it quite a while and it wasn't new when he bought it so, from the outside, it looked a little battered. But inside it was as snug as could be. He kept it in half of Dr. Bolton's garage and, as Judy had often told him jokingly, she could keep tabs on everything he did. Now she wouldn't want to. But she couldn't help being thankful Peter was free this afternoon.

"Mrs. Piper broke her appointment," Judy explained bluntly. "The salesman probably convinced her it wasn't necessary to have us go along and see the lot."

"Clever salesman!" Peter remarked. "He must have guessed what you girls are up to."

"I wish I knew exactly what we are up to," Honey said.

"I wish I did too," Judy agreed. "There are so many things people don't want to tell. Even Mrs. Piper——"

"She's the worst of all."

"I don't think so, Honey," Judy contradicted her. But her accusing glance was lost on Peter. He was not in the mood for quarreling although Judy did feel a certain tension between them. Besides, he had his eyes on the road, driving as

fast as he dared along the winding route over
the mountain and down into Dry Brook Hollow.
Judy's grandparents lived there but this time
they did not stop. The place was too far from
the road for Judy to see the old folks as she
passed it. But she did see Red, the boy who did
the farm work now that her grandfather was
too feeble. She noticed that he was setting out
trees on the hillside. The trees would be trans-
planted, later, when he began his landscape
gardening in Roulsville. For Red, too, had been
promised work with the Ace Building Company.
Judy wondered who would improve these lots
that the Roulsville Development Company were
giving away.

"I wonder if many people won lots," she said.
"If they did, I don't see why we didn't unless——"

"Unless what?" Honey asked when Judy
paused, her eyes on Peter.

"Unless we weren't classed as suckers," Judy
finished emphatically.

It was only a short drive from Dry Brook
Hollow to Roulsville. They came into the town
on a road built along a bank so that they could
see the town before they got there. The new
paper mill was already sending forth clouds of

steam from its busy machinery and there were piles and piles of timber ready to be made into paper pulp. The radio factory wasn't quite finished and the homes the Ace Building Company were putting up were mere skeletons of beams and studding. Beyond these there was a field which originally had been used as a cow pasture but now had a rough road going through it. Judy noted in astonishment that the road was an extension of her own Judy Lane. Several expensive-looking cars were parked along this road.

"I bet you those are the free lots and those nifty cars belong to the salesman," Judy observed as she peered eagerly out the open window of Peter's car. "See the people walking around. They're looking at something and there's nothing much to see but the land they're walking on."

"It's good land," Peter said. "They're not being cheated on the land if those are the lots the Roulsville Development Company is giving away."

"It might be an honest business," Honey put in hopefully.

"Not much chance of it," Peter said. "We simply haven't found the catch. If it had been

honest there wouldn't have been so many winners.''

"And we would have come with the salesman,'' Judy added, "not with Peter. Look!
This is the place. There's Mrs. Piper now!''

The woman ran forward, not a bit surprised
that Judy and her friends should be there. In
fact, she seemed to be expecting them.

"My, you're late!'' she exclaimed when Peter
drove into the parking space. "I've been waiting for you nearly an hour. But it's all right,''
she continued, waving their objections aside,
"the lot is mine. I've paid for the deed and
now it's free and clear and there are no strings
to it at all. The salesman has just been showing
me around.''

"You paid for the deed!'' Peter exclaimed.
"How much did they soak you?''

Mrs. Piper hesitated. "Only twenty-five dollars—to make it legal,'' she explained. "The
salesman said it was necessary in order to have
the property deeded to me. People do pay legal
fees, don't they? I—I do want the lot and—and
twenty-five dollars isn't much, though it was
supposed to last the month,'' she finished lamely.
"My husband's mother just sent it.''

"Swindlers! And we weren't in time to stop

them. But I'll see you get your land,'' Peter declared, ''if I have to shovel it, piece by piece, down that salesman's throat.''

''Could we see the lot?'' Honey ventured at last.

''I don't see why not,'' Mrs. Piper replied, ''although there's nothing much to see but land and one big shade tree. There it is!'' She pointed. ''There where that big maple tree stands. The lot goes back for a hundred feet beyond the maple.''

''A hundred feet!'' Judy exclaimed. ''Why, that's a fairly generous slice of land for a lot in town. But how wide is it, Mrs. Piper?''

''How wide is it?''

''Yes. How wide is the lot? You say it goes back a hundred feet. But I was just wondering if your lot is wide enough to build a house on.''

CHAPTER VI

A FIFTEEN FOOT LOT

THE width of the lot remained a puzzle while Mrs. Piper went hunting her salesman. She couldn't remember that he said anything about how wide it was.

"But he was awfully nice about it," she finished.

He continued to be "awfully nice."

"That's his business," Peter remarked grimly.

He was a man Judy had not seen at the garden party and yet his voice sounded exactly like the voice that had said, "Look out for suckers." Immediately the thought flashed across Judy's mind, "He may be Horace's Mr. X."

His speech was almost as polished as that of the limerick singer. It was clear that he was used to wriggling out of things. He had his piece learned well.

"This woman was unfortunate enough to win a rather narrow lot," he explained. "She could build on it, of course. But for a really fine house she must have a little more land. Our company is willing to sell the adjoining lot at a reasonable figure and we have contracted a building company who will furnish plans and take care of all the details of construction. I have a book here if you would care to see it,'' he added, turning to Mrs. Piper. ''You say you want a large house with a wide porch——''

''But not larger than the lot. We couldn't afford——''

''Very well,'' he interrupted, flipping the pages of a book he had taken from his car, ''I'll be glad to show you a more modest house than the one I had originally intended showing you. This little frame dwelling with the brick front is built on a twenty foot lot.''

''It's so narrow,'' Mrs. Piper remarked, looking at the picture.

''Not at all. There's a living room fifteen by fifteen and a nine by twelve dining room and a kitchenette on the first floor. That is in addition to the sun parlor. Or,'' he continued blandly, ''you could have an open porch.''

''I'd rather. That will be all right, I guess,'' she decided uncertainly, ''if it's possible to get a loan. Could Mr. Dobbs see to that?''

"We take care of the loans," the salesman answered. "It will cost you only twenty dollars a month to have such a house built. And you won't need to pay a cent extra once you have paid for the lot."

"But the lot was free!"

"I mean the adjoining lot you will need if you build this particular house."

"You mean my lot isn't big enough even for this little house?" Mrs. Piper exclaimed in dismay. "Then what kind of a house can I build without buying more land?"

But in the meantime Judy and Peter had been looking at the contract Mrs. Piper had signed and had found the words, *a piece of land fifteen by one hundred feet.*

"A fifteen foot lot!" Peter said in disgust. "So this is the racket. You might make a little money on this deal, Mrs. Piper, if you built a lunch car on your lot. It's just about wide enough for a lunch car."

"But," she protested, "I want a home—not a lunch car."

"My dear woman! Of course you want a home. And for thirty dollars a month," the salesman said, "you can have it. And it's still cheaper than rent."

"Thirty dollars a month for how long?" Judy put in.

"Until the adjoining lot is paid for."

"And how long will that be?"

"Such payments," he explained, "usually extend over quite a period of time. But we will not foreclose the mortgage as long as the payments are kept up. Mrs. Piper needn't worry about that. She needn't worry about anything. We'll see that she has a fine house on a thirty by one hundred foot lot for only thirty dollars a month."

Mrs. Piper smiled. "It does sound reasonable," she said. "You see, Miss Bolton, they're really saving money for me."

"Exactly," the salesman beamed.

Saving money by taking Mrs. Piper's last cent to pay for a deed to a lot that was supposed to be free! Saving money by hanging a mortgage over her head—a mortgage that could be foreclosed at a moment's notice if hard luck came again and she was not able to pay the required thirty dollars a month! And even at that she was paying for a house that was still too small to be much of a home. It wasn't Judy's idea of saving.

"You won't decide on the house until you've

talked it over with us, will you?'' she asked anxiously.

''No,'' Mrs. Piper replied, still a little uncertain, ''I do believe it will be better to talk it over. But I don't want to bother my husband about it. A new house would be such a nice surprise!''

''We'll think about it then,'' Peter put in. ''You're going back in my car, Mrs. Piper, if Mr. —'' he paused, waiting for the salesman to give his name.

The man was silent.

''If Mr. X, here, will let you have the deed to your lot,'' Peter finished.

The salesman fumbled about, apparently searching for it. ''Oh, yes. Of course, the deed,'' he stammered. ''I must have mislaid it. If you'll excuse me a minute I'll look in my car——''

''No, you don't!'' Peter cried, swinging him around and facing his belligerently. ''You'll look for it in your left hip pocket right where I saw you put it when Mrs. Piper decided not to buy the adjoining lot. Now may I have the deed?''

To Judy's utter amazement, the salesman handed the legal document to Peter.

"Now if you girls are ready," the young lawyer said, "I think we'll go home."

He walked along with Mrs. Piper and Algie, who had been having a grand time climbing trees and romping on the grass. But Honey pulled Judy back.

"Wasn't Peter splendid?" she whispered. "Now aren't you proud of him?"

"I am proud," Judy said. But her eyes were troubled as she added, "I wish I knew . . ."

On the way home Peter explained the law and this time everybody listened most attentively. What was wrong and what was legally wrong appeared to be two entirely different propositions.

"There's no charge you can prefer against a firm like the Roulsville Development Company. They're sharpers and swindlers and racketeers. But they're operating within the law. The little act you witnessed today was as crooked as the letter S but there was nothing illegal about it. They raffled off land, but not enough land to build on. That gives them an excellent chance to sell the adjoining lots at a higher figure than they would otherwise bring. Even the advance fee was technically within the law and, if the salesman hadn't known I might try to take the deed by force and cause a row, he probably never would have given it to me. You see,'' Peter pointed out, ''they don't want trouble. But they have it all fixed so that the law will be on their side if they can't keep out of it. I believe they can be beaten but a lawyer can't do it alone. The people who win the lots must help. That's why I suggested the lunch car.''

''But a lunch car way out there in the fields! It wouldn't make any money.''

''No,'' Peter admitted, ''I'm afraid it wouldn't. But it was the only thing I could think of that might be built on a fifteen foot lot.''

''We could build a house for my chicken,'' Algie spoke up. And everybody laughed—a little ruefully perhaps. For there was truth in what Algie said. A chicken coop, a lunch car, a dog kennel maybe. But certainly not the home Mrs. Piper wanted on a lot only fifteen feet wide.

They discussed it all the way home. Judy was shocked to learn that companies like the Roulsville Development Company paid their lawyers for drawing up crooked contracts that would still be within the law.

"That's how some lawyers make their money," Peter declared, "but I'd starve before I'd make a red penny that way."

"You might defend these people that have been swindled," Judy said.

But Peter was afraid he'd never have the chance. "They won't bring suit. The salesmen will make this look like a good thing and the people will fall for it."

"Just like I would have fallen today if you hadn't been there," Mrs. Piper put in. "I was almost afraid you weren't coming."

Peter grinned. "I guess you expected us to follow you. What did the salesman say? Wasn't there room in the car?"

"There really wasn't," she answered. "He had another family along besides ours. The Bradys. They said they knew you. I think they won a lot too."

"I hope they don't want it," Peter said. "I'll buy it of them."

"You?" Judy asked. "What on earth for?"

"It would be convenient to have a law office on one of these fifteen foot lots. A brick building that size would be plenty large enough for me. Yes," Peter decided, "I will see the Bradys unless Mrs. Piper wants to sell her lot."

"But I don't. I want to live on it. I wish somebody could advise me what to do."

Judy wished she could be that somebody. She returned from the ride still trying to plan something. She sat for a while in the hammock by herself, with just Blackberry for company, and then went in and told the family all about it. She felt better when Horace promised to expose the racket in his paper.

"If you could think of some good publicity stunt," he suggested. "Peter's lunch car idea isn't bad. But I mean some really novel thing to do with the lot that will sort of show them up." He waved his hand with a fork in it and a string bean on the end of the fork. They were discussing the thing at dinner table with Judy's father and mother as an interested audience. "You know," he continued, "something people will talk about. Something other people who have been swindled in the same way might imitate. You couldn't have a row of lunch wagons for people to live in, could you? That's the general idea."

Judy thought a minute, tracing fork lines through her mashed potatoes. Horace's suggestion was good. In fact, as she thought harder, she decided it was very good. By the time she had finished dessert, it was excellent. She jumped up from the table, eyes alight.

"I have it!" she cried. "They've sold Mrs. Piper half a lot. Why couldn't she build half a house on it? I'm sure Arthur could design something with an eye to completing it later on when Mrs. Piper can afford to buy the extra land. You see, with half a house there, they won't be able to sell the adjoining lot to anybody else. We'll be beating them at their own game. Come, Horace," Judy begged. "Let's go down and see Arthur tonight. Honey thinks she can depend on her brother and I'm sure now that I can depend on mine."

"Gee, Sis! It sounds good," the young reporter said in admiration as he gulped down the rest of his coffee and excused himself from the table.

The doctor sighed and put down his coffee cup too. "I wish I could go at my work with that enthusiasm," he said.

"How is the little patient?" Mrs. Bolton asked.

"No better. But if anything can save her, those blood transfusions will. We're still hoping."

CHAPTER VII

HALF A HOUSE

"It's impossible," Arthur said when Judy had finished outlining her idea. "You couldn't possibly build more than a one or two room cottage on a lot that size. A two story building would look queer."

"That's what we want. The queerer the house looks the better publicity we can give it," Horace said.

"But what about Mrs. Piper?" Judy asked. "We're doing this for her and she won't want to live in a freak house. No, Arthur, it must be attractive. Couldn't you design some sort of attractive little two story cottage fifteen feet wide?"

"It couldn't be that wide," Arthur objected. "The most you have to build your foundation on is twelve to thirteen feet. Remember, unless you're building a brick structure with a slanting roof, you have to allow for the eaves. They can't jut over onto the adjoining lot."

"I hadn't thought of that."

"You couldn't have a peak roof on a two story house twelve feet wide," Arthur went on, "it would make the roof too steep. The peak would look like a tower."

"Like the funny little houses in Mother Goose."

"Exactly," he agreed. "But hard to work on. How are you going to get men to shingle a roof that's practically straight up and down?"

"But if you built the house the other way?"

Arthur considered this a moment. "It would still look queer. But, at least, it's plausible." He took a sheet of paper and began sketching the house roughly. "Yes," he said, viewing his sketch, "we might do that. Then, later, when the house is completed, this affair we're planning would become the right wing."

Just then Lois and Lorraine, arm in arm as usual, walked into the room.

"Hello, Judy!" they greeted her. "Hello, Horace! What's Arthur talking about? Not the chicken we had for dinner? I had no idea he wanted the right wing."

"It isn't a chicken," laughed Judy. "It's a house. Will there be a left wing too—later on?"

"There might be," Arthur replied. "This

type of house might have any number of additions built onto it. But I still think it looks odd just by itself.''

Lois and Lorraine bent over the paper to see.

''So that's a wing, is it?'' Lois laughed. ''It looks almost thin enough to fly.''

''Don't make fun of it,'' Judy whispered. ''He might decide we couldn't build it and then we would be in a jam. By the way,'' she asked in a louder tone, ''neither you nor Lorraine won lots, did you?''

''Indeed we didn't.''

''I guess none of us were suckers,'' Judy said mysteriously. For she had told no one of the mistaken directions she had received at the garden party.

Horace looked at her curiously. ''It doesn't sound nice to call anyone a sucker,'' he said righteously. ''Dad wouldn't like to hear you using such language.''

Lois and Lorraine also seemed shocked by the word.

''Just the same,'' Judy declared, ''some people are suckers. We can be glad we aren't. But, you know,'' she confided, ''it would be fun to be thought a sucker and then not really be one. Wouldn't I love the chance!''

"Dear only knows what you're talking about," Lois said.

Arthur looked annoyed. He hated to appear ridiculous and this half house Judy was so set on having him design was beginning to look like a piece of little girl foolishness.

"I've changed my mind," he said suddenly. "It's not practicable to build such a house. Don't you realize, Judy, that there would be no space for even so much as a path around to the back? Every time you walked around to the back of the house you'd be trespassing on somebody else's land."

"You wouldn't need to walk around the house. You could walk through it."

"Even so, it's inviting trouble. I won't chance it."

"Very well. I'll design the house myself. But if I do," Judy pleaded, "won't you just go over the plans and see that they're right? I don't know about wall space—I mean how thick to make the walls and all that. And I wouldn't know about windows."

"If you're going to have an addition on it later it would be a waste of time and material to put any windows in it at all. The left side of your house will be the wall between your wing and your main building. You'd have to do without doors too for if you had them you'd not be able to use them. That, again, would be trespassing."

"Oh, dear!" Judy sighed. "How complicated this all is."

"Do you still want to design the house yourself?" Arthur asked.

Judy glanced at her brother and there was a boyish twinkle in his eye. Lois and Lorraine were huddled together, their eyes wide, waiting to hear what Judy would say. Arthur was tapping the table with the eraser end of his pencil.

"Yes," Judy said. "I still want to design the house. I think it will be fun."

Late that evening Judy worked over the plans. She wouldn't let anybody else help her, not even Mrs. Piper.

"I'll draw the plans," she had told the woman over the telephone, "and then if you don't like them, we'll change them together."

"Remember the porch."

"Yes, a wide one with lattice work."

"And I want a fireplace," Mrs. Piper had reminded her. "Don't you think a house is cozy with a fireplace so you can light a fire cold winter evenings?"

"Ye-es," Judy had replied uncertainly. She was still wondering how on earth she'd fit a fireplace and porch both into the tiny, narrow house she had sketched somewhat after Arthur's drawing. In the sketch the house was quite bare and ugly. One whole side was without windows and the low, sloping roof left room for only a door in front. The porch brought the roof lower still. It looked more as though it were intended for a slide in a playground than the front of anybody's house. Judy puzzled over it awhile. She tried putting a little window each side of the front door but there really wasn't room. She tried a door and a window side by side but that didn't look right either. It made the whole house one-sided when she changed the steps and placed them before the door where they naturally ought to be. Erasing it all, she put the door back in the center exactly where it was before. She held the sketch away from her and looked at it critically. Hopeless! Arthur wouldn't even help her correct a drawing like that. She was almost in tears over her efforts when Peter rang the bell.

"Felt like talking with somebody," he explained. "Got any more ideas about Mrs. Piper's lot?"

Judy sighed. "This," she said, thrusting the badly drawn sketch before his eyes.

"Wow!" he exclaimed. "What's this, the broad side of a chicken coop?"

"It looks like it. I can't get it to come right. Do look at it, Peter, and tell me what's the matter."

"Your perspective is cock-eyed, for one thing," Peter began, eyeing the sketch with a critical squint. "What's the matter with putting a few windows on the left side of the house?"

"We can't. There's going to be an addition."

"A little dormer up here in front might improve the looks of it then."

"A dormer window? Of course!" Judy exclaimed. "But I don't know how to draw anything," she lamented. "I'd be ashamed to let Arthur see this thing."

"Poor Judy!" Peter was grinning that dear, impish grin that Judy had loved ever since they were boy and girl together. "Talented in everything but drawing! Little detective, will you quit trying to be an architect and let Honey draw the picture for you?"

A grateful smile was on Judy's face as she looked up at him. He hadn't said, "Let Arthur

draw it.'' He hadn't even asked her why Arthur wasn't drawing the plans in the first place.
''He's more charitable than I am,'' she thought.
''I wish I could forget Miss Ames. But I just
can't. Probably she's busy and that's why he's
here tonight.''

But she told him she'd love to have Honey
draw the picture and the three of them worked
and puzzled over it the next evening until even
Judy was satisfied. She solved the fireplace
problem by placing the chimney on the outside.
That took the barren look away from the windowless side of the house and later, when the
addition was built on, the chimney would go up
through the center of the house and allow for
two, or even four fireplaces if Mrs. Piper wanted
them.

Judy planned the house with a living room,
breakfast room and kitchen downstairs and two
bedrooms and a bath on the second floor. Of
course the house did look long and it did look
very narrow but, the way Honey drew it, it was
really an attractive place. From the porch to
the back door it was fifty feet long. That left
fifty more feet for the grounds in front and
back.

''Algie's chicken can have this twenty-five

foot piece in back to scratch in and Mrs. Piper can grow flowers in the other twenty-five feet,'' Judy decided as she looked over the drawing. Honey had even sketched in the tree. It was very close to the front of the house.

"Like our tree," Judy said. "It will shade the porch."

"It's going to be wonderfully cool," Honey said.

"A little too cool, I'm afraid, with only one fireplace to heat the whole house. Perhaps we ought to put another one upstairs. I really think we ought," Judy finally decided, "right here in the largest bedroom."

"Well," Peter said, sitting back in his chair with his thumbs in his knitted zipper vest, "we've built the house on paper anyway. My office is built on paper too. Mrs. Brady's lot was just down the street from Mrs. Piper's and I did succeed in getting it deeded to me. But that's only the beginning."

"Arthur thinks we'll have trouble," Judy ventured.

Peter's eyes twinkled. "Trouble," he repeated, taking both Judy's hands and squeezing them with an enthusiasm that hurt. "Trouble? Yes, and don't we love it!"

CHAPTER VIII

A THREATENING NOTE

ARTHUR corrected the plans, just as he had promised, after Mrs. Piper had approved them. But the Ace Building Company refused to have anything to do with either Peter's office or the little house Judy had designed. "Playing with fire" they called it. And, in this instance, the "fire" was their rival, the Roulsville Development Company, who employed their own builders.

"I'll have to get some simple carpenter," Judy decided, "after Peter has arranged a loan."

John Olsen was the simplest carpenter she could find. He was a Swede with a flat, childlike face and stiff blonde hair a little gray at the temples. John Olsen was the kind of man who would carry a job through to the finish but when Judy saw his crew of men she wasn't so sure about them. He had four, at first. An older man and his son and two middle-aged brothers with rather bristly beards and baggy, khaki trousers. Peter said they looked like a gang of crooks, all but "faithful John." But Judy thought they looked more life shiftless, no-account bums who found it hard to keep a job because they had no great liking for work. The bricklayers working on Peter's office building were of quite a different sort. The building was finished before Mrs. Piper's house was fairly started.

Things began to go wrong almost at once. The men kept losing their tools and having to substitute others. They never saw anyone take them. But the minute they laid them down— presto! They were gone. It wasn't faithful John who came to Judy with the complaint. It was the two bristly bearded brothers.

"There's spooks around the place, that's what," they declared. "It ain't only that the tools disappear. But that whistling is driving us nuts. Like something flying through the air, it is. I always was agin the idea of workin' in a ghost town."

Those two were "agin the idea" of working anywhere, Judy decided. If they did get scared and quit, John would accomplish just as much without them. "*Ghost town* is just a name," she said. "If you keep close watch I'm sure you'll see those spooks you complain of. They'll be flesh-and-blood real estate men. They're trying to stop us from building the house."

"I was right," Judy observed the next morning when she saw two large NO TRESPASS-ING signs posted on the lots on either side of Mrs. Piper's house. The Roulsville Develop-ment Company's men had figured it out that if they put up those signs the workmen would be unable to build their scaffolding on the side of the house and hence could not complete it. But John had been told of the possible trouble and his scaffolding was so narrow that not a beam of it extended onto the other property.

"They'll have to do some trespassing them-selves if they want to stop my men," he declared.

"That's possible too," Judy laughed. "Only they'd better not be caught at it."

She told Peter and he posted a NO TRES-PASSING sign on Mrs. Piper's lot also.

The framework of the house was up now. Judy spent a great deal of time in Roulsville watching the men work and listening to the mu-sic of their hammers. To her it was very real music. "Going up! Going up!" the hammers seemed to say. At the rate the men were working the house would be completed in almost no time.

But Judy couldn't be in Roulsville every day. She was just finishing up a business course she had decided to take at Peter's suggestion and, now that the Easter vacation was over, she had examinations to take in both shorthand and typing before she would be qualified for a position.

Honey, too, had gone back to school. Sylvia Weiss had stopped for her. (Sylvia had spent the week visiting relatives in Cleveland) and they had gone back to New York together. Judy missed Honey and she missed Peter on his mysterious "nights out" but she had promised herself that she would trust him and so she asked no questions. She could even forget about Miss Ames when she and Peter became deeply interested in something and now they were both deeply interested in his law office and Mrs. Piper's house.

The law office had gone up much faster than the house. This bothered Judy. John and his men were being well paid. Why couldn't they hurry—before something happened to stop them? And then, one day when Judy came to Roulsville with Peter, she noticed the men had stopped working. Not a soul was around.

"Some of those real estate people have made them quit," she decided at once and walked belligerently around to John Olsen's house. John was in bed with a sudden attack of asthma.

"It gets me like this—sudden," he explained between sneezes. "But the other men ought to be working. They gave me their word they'd stick it out."

"Was it so hard then?" Judy asked.

"Something scared them," he said, "though I don't know what it was. Some noise, I guess. None of us saw anything. The house is too close to that blooming race track."

"Race track!" Judy exclaimed. "I didn't know there was a race track."

"There must be," John said, "we keep hearing horses."

"But you're not afraid of horses, are you?"

"Not me. But the men are. They're scared to death of horses they can't see. They call them ghost horses."

"Ghost horses in a ghost town! They need a boss to keep them steady. I'll have my father give you an inoculation for asthma and you'll be as well as ever," Judy promised.

The inoculation did all that was expected of it. But work on the house had been delayed almost a week. Meanwhile Peter was having difficulties in his law office. Some night prowler had broken in all the window panes.

"It will soon be summer," Peter said cheerfully, "and I won't need windows except to keep the mosquitoes out."

So he put up screens in place of the glassed-in windows and when it rained through the screens he patiently mopped the floor of his new office. He had no furniture, as yet, except a battered oak desk and a swivel chair and a cot that sat too far away from the windows for the rain to reach.

"I could sleep on the cot," he said, "if it came to that, and catch the prowler in the act of prowling."

"I'd like to catch our prowler," Judy rejoined. "The men have been missing their tools again and they still talk of ghost horses. We know there isn't any race track in Roulsville. I'd like to hear those horses. I bet I could tell what they are."

She and Peter were walking in the direction of Mrs. Piper's new house as they talked. It was only a short distance away from Peter's office. Both were on the new extension of Judy Lane and Judy still thrilled to the thought whenever she happened to remember that their street was really named for her.

"I like to think of the whole street lined with beautiful houses something like Mrs. Piper's will be when it has its other wing," she said.

"I'd like to think of the whole street lined with dinky little narrow buildings with vacant lots in between," Peter returned. "That's what it's got to be lined with if we're going to beat this real estate racket. Some of the people who won lots are going to take the matter to court and have the ownership of the property established by court decree."

"Whatever that means."

"It means," Peter said, "that the winners of these lots present their letters from the Roulsville Development Company to a court as proof that they own the land. They're acting on my advice and if the court decrees that the property is theirs that settles it, once and forever. You see, I'm not there every time to take possession of the deed and that's the only way these other winners can get hold of it."

"I begin to see," Judy said. "You're doing a big thing, Peter. And if we can finish this house and if other people build houses like it . . ."

It was a big dream, a dream of a new Roulsville—truly the resurrection of a ghost town. Peter and Judy were lost in the wonder of imagining it. Not until they were almost there did they notice anything strange about Mrs. Piper's house.

"What is it?" Judy gasped when she did notice. "Look, Peter! Look!"

John, his hammer in his hand, was standing before the corner stud of the house reading something that was written there in red letters. It looked as though it were written with red paint—or blood. Judy shuddered as this gruesome thought presented itself to her. She and Peter came nearer.

"What is it, John?"

"It's a warning, by George! But they can't scare me."

"Did the other workmen see it?" Judy asked.

"They were all reading it," he replied. "But I sent them back to their jobs so I could figure it out for myself. What do you suppose the red circle is, Miss Judy?"

The Red Circle!

Judy looked more closely at the warning.

BEWARE OF THE RED CIRCLE, it said. But all around it were tiny rings of blood red.

For sheer horror, Judy thought, a skull and crossbones would have been far less effective. The circles weren't an even red but were dotted on, probably with the point of a nail. Sometimes there were two circles, one within another. But none of the circles were any larger than a five-cent piece.

"I saw some little boys prowling around here, Miss Judy. I chased them away with a yard ruler."

"That's right, John," Judy said bravely. "This is probably some of their mischief."

But she and Peter both knew the mysterious threat was the work of something far more dangerous than little boys. The Red Circle! Probably a name for a secret society organized by the real estate people on purpose to scare the workmen away.

"Guess they don't know much about your reputation for solving spooky things," Peter said to Judy after she had told him her theory. He agreed. It probably was a gang of real estate men and not half as dangerous as it sounded.

"But no matter what it is," he finished, "it can't be any worse than some of the mysteries we've solved before. Better get old Blackberry on the job to help you."

CHAPTER IX

THE RED CIRCLE STRIKES

BLACKBERRY, now a long, lean, middle-aged cat, had seen a great deal of adventure in his life. But, unlike the black cat in all the superstitious stories one hears, he had brought Judy so much good luck that she often thought of him as her mascot. He had been with her in camp in the Thousand Islands and had flown home with her from New York in the beautiful airplane that used to be Arthur's proudest possession. Once Blackberry had saved Judy's life. And so it was natural that Peter should suggest the cat's presence in Roulsville when the mysteries around Mrs. Piper's unfinished house were beginning to deepen.

"I'll leave him with the workmen to bring them luck," Judy announced as she climbed into Peter's car with the cat in her arms.

Mrs. Piper and Algie and Algie's pet chicken were riding to Roulsville with Peter the same day Judy decided to take Blackberry. In the few weeks he had owned it the chicken had grown from a fluffy, soft ball to a rather awkward, long-legged, half naked rooster. Fluff, its original name, now seemed hopelessly out of place. Pinfeathers would have been more like it. But Algie loved Fluff and still insisted he was a handsome chicken. Quite without meaning to, Peter had sent the little boy off into another fit of hysterics by remarking, as a joke, "He's almost big enough for a fricassee."

Now Algie sat in a corner of the back seat, almost crushing his chicken by holding it so tightly. Judy, with her cat, sat in front. Occasionally, when she wasn't minding him, Blackberry looked back with a spiteful *Ffft!* For Blackberry hated chickens almost as much as he hated dogs. He was dog-like himself in many ways. A strange step outside the door would cause him to sit up at attention. He had a dog's affection for Judy. But just let anyone say the word "dog" in his presence and his back would arch and bristle and his tail become the size of an old-fashioned feather boa.

For several days now, Mrs. Piper had been wanting to see her new house. Naturally, Algie wanted to see it and he insisted on taking the chicken along and leaving it in its new yard.

Mrs. Piper smiled as she explained, "I thought it might be a good idea too. I've heard of men having all sorts of things for mascots. So why not a chicken?"

Judy's eyes grew bigger. "So you were bringing it for a mascot? How strange! I was bringing Blackberry along for the same reason."

"I don't know what Blackberry could do," Peter said, "but then, we didn't know what Blackberry could do the other times he helped us, did we, Judy?"

"Indeed we didn't," she agreed. "But we found out all right when he knocked the gun out of Slippery McQuirk's hand and dug his way down to that trap door in our cellar. Even when he was a kitten he helped us solve mysteries. Remember, Peter?"

"Sure I remember. Good old Blackberry!" And Peter put out one hand to stroke the cat's neck as he drove the car with the other.

"Watch out!" Judy cried. "There's somebody trying to pass us."

"It's that limerick singer," Mrs. Piper said. "I wonder where he's bound for."

"Roulsville, the same as we are. He's one of the Roulsville Development Company's salesmen. Or at least I think he is," Judy added. "But I don't see any customers with him."

"More trouble," Peter prophesied grimly.

He found it as soon as he reached his office. Somebody had thrown a stone through the window directly into his ink well. It took a little while to mend the screen and clean up the ink spatters and Judy and Mrs. Piper helped while Algie held his chicken at a safe distance from Blackberry. Peter suggested leaving the cat at the office but Judy had made up her mind. She carried Blackberry and Algie carried his chicken as they walked on toward the new house.

Judy knew something was wrong when Blackberry's tail began to bristle. It was more than the chicken this time. He smelt dog and before Judy could stop him he was out of her arms and away.

"Bad cat! Bad cat!" Algie screamed as Blackberry made straight for the house. The hammering stopped as a black torpedo darted past the workmen and on into the back yard where the cat's dog-enemy was tied. He flew at the dog and black and spotted fur flew. One of the workmen was well scratched before Judy could pull the fighting animals apart.

"I'm so sorry," she apologized. "I know he hates dogs but I didn't think you had one here."

"A man sold him to us this morning for luck," the workman explained. "And we sure need it in this hole."

"That is a joke on me," Judy laughed. "I was bringing the cat for luck and this little boy was bringing the chicken. Now look what happens! The dog is such a quiet animal too, exactly like a dog I had at the pet booth at the garden party."

"That was Spottie," Algie announced. "He used to be my dog but my mommie gave him to the hospital 'cause I didn't like him."

"We all like him," the workman said, patting the animal's head as he talked.

The dog looked up at Judy.

"My goodness!" she exclaimed. "He is the same dog. His spots are just the same and he's only a little larger. He could have grown that much in a month."

Algie had walked off without a backward look at the dog he said used to be his. It seemed strange to Judy that the boy shouldn't have more affection for a former pet. He appeared to be so fond of his chicken.

"How's the house coming along?" she asked. "It looks nearly finished."

The plasterers were at work inside, making everything white and dusty. The windows and doors were yet to be put in and it was still necessary to walk into the house along a plank as the front porch was not completed.

"Looks like we'll be done the end of the week if all goes well," John told her.

All seemed to be going well at the moment. Judy looked about her with a feeling of satisfaction. It was Mrs. Piper's house but it was her idea and so, in a sense, it was her house also. Algie had found some sawed-off ends of wood and was busy building things on the floor. Mrs. Piper was asking questions of the workmen and the chicken was scratching contentedly in the yard. So Judy slipped quietly out of the door and took Blackberry back to Peter.

"Surprise!" she called out at the door of his office. "Nothing happened worse than a cat fight and the men already have a mascot, thank you, so they won't need Blackberry. We'll keep him here today and tonight we can take him home."

"Look here, Judy! They've installed my new telephone. The men just left. Now this is a real office. I wonder who will be the first person to call.''

''Oh, let me be!'' Judy cried. ''I'll run down town to the drug store and ring you up right away before anybody else gets ahead of me.''

But Judy stopped for a soda first. Then she went into a booth, deposited her nickel, and dialed Peter's number. She listened. There was a buzzing noise over the wire. A busy signal! Oh, dear! If only she hadn't taken the time for that soda she could have been first. Now it was somebody else. Perhaps Miss Ames. But Judy hated herself for the thought. Peter's telephone was put in his office for business calls.

In a minute or two Judy dialed again and this time Peter's voice sounded clearly over the wire.

''Too late,'' he said. ''Somebody else called first. And who do you think it was?''

''I can't imagine.''

''It was one of those two lazy brothers. You know, the ones who are working on Mrs. Piper's house. And they gave me the strangest message. They said, 'Tell John the Red Circle's got us' and then they hung up. What do you think I ought to do about it?''

''I suppose you'll have to tell John.''

''But how could the Red Circle get them? If

it had them, how could they telephone? And what is this confounded Red Circle anyway?"

"I wish I knew. I'll stop off and give John the message," Judy promised, "and see how he takes it."

John took it as calmly as could be expected under the circumstances.

"I knew we were headed for trouble," he said. "I knew it the minute I read that ghastly red warning on the stud. Now all my men will quit. But I can finish up alone," he declared bravely. "I'm no quitter. It's got to be something bigger than ghosts to scare me out of a job."

"Why do you say ghosts?"

"Because, Miss Judy, we've been hearing horses again. And there ain't any real horses around here. This Red Circle comes riding on horses—invisible horses—ghost horses! Don't ask me to explain it. I ain't spooky or anything like that. I just know horses when I hear 'em and every time we hear those horses there's more trouble. It will take more than a spotted dog to bring luck to this house."

"How is the dog?" Judy asked.

"Sick. The blasted dog hasn't wanted to stand on his feet since your cat went at him.

And Mrs. Piper and the boy have gone. Chicken too. They lit out of here like something being chased when we commenced to hear those horses.''

''Where did they go? Did they tell you?''

''Nope. Didn't say a word. Just lit out. Likely they went back to that lawyer's office.''

''I'll see.''

And Judy hurried back to Peter's office, wishing all the time that she had been the one to hear the ghostly horses. Or Horace. What a newspaper story Horace could make of this when she told him! She didn't suppose it was very funny to those who were being frightened. But nobody could say it wasn't exciting.

Blackberry met her when she opened the office door. He was all alone.

Judy caught her breath. What could have happened to Peter? But then she saw a note under a paper weight on his desk. She read:

Dear Judy: I've gone to take Mrs. Piper home. She and Algie were both hysterical. Wait here with Blackberry until I return and don't lose your head if anything happens. I'm depending on you.

PETER

CHAPTER X

"Now what could happen?" Judy wondered as she sat alone in the office waiting. "I suppose the ghost horses might come riding to get me. But I'd know what they were. And if I didn't, I'd find out. I always have."

She was confident this mystery, like all the others, had a logical explanation. The Red Circle sounded frightening enough. But it couldn't be anything but a secret society or, at the very worst, an organized gang. Certainly it was nothing supernatural. It was too well timed for that. Spirits, Judy knew, could not be in league with the real estate people. And these ghost horses were.

"I wish I'd hear them," Judy kept thinking.

But there was no sound in the office at all. It was almost too still when Judy's thoughts were so busy. If Peter had not told her to wait she would have gone out for a walk.

She was growing a little drowsy, trying to

puzzle it all out and having so little success. She leaned back in Peter's swivel chair. She'd just rest there until Peter came and then perhaps they'd go out to dinner together and talk things over. But the swivel chair was too hard. She couldn't rest there. She tried the cot and before she knew what was happening she was off in the land of dreams. She had been thinking of horses when she fell asleep so now she dreamed of horses. But they were beautiful horses with plumes on their heads and knights in armor were riding . . . riding . . . One black horse was ahead. It seemed there'd been a race and this black horse . . . no, cat . . . It was a black cat and it was scratching on the door. Why, it was Blackberry and Judy had been asleep! How long, she wondered. Did Peter have a clock? Her wrist watch had stopped. Its hands pointed to six. It ought to be dark now. She looked out the window. Why, it was just beginning to be light! The horizon was still tinted with yellow. The sun was just rising. Judy realized she had slept in Peter's office all night *and Peter had not come!*

"Something has happened to him!" she spoke aloud to Blackberry.

The cat meowed his sympathy.

"I've got to get home," Judy continued, still speaking aloud. "What'll we do, Blackberry? Who will take us?"

She gathered the cat in her arms and stepped out into the dim morning. It was cold and misty. Roulsville looked like only the shadow of a town. Not a car was moving along the deserted streets. Judy thought of the unfinished house. The workmen would be there early and perhaps one of them could help her. John had a car. In an emergency like this he would be glad to drive her home.

As Judy neared the house she could hear the rhythmic sound of a hammer—no, a pick. Some-one was digging. And it was still too early for the men to be at work. This was ghastly. For the first time, a very real fear took possession of Judy. Suppose that someone should be in-visible—like the horses? How could she explain that? Screwing up all her courage and holding Blackberry closer, she walked up the narrow plank and into the house. But the digging was beyond the house—in the yard. It was a real sound. Thank Heaven! It was a real person. It was John.

"John!" Judy exclaimed.

He turned on his heel, wiping one grimy hand

across his forehead. He squinted at Judy through the mist.

"Miss Judy! What are you doing here?"

She tried to make light of the question. She attempted a laugh.

"That's just what I was going to ask you."

"The dog died," he said simply. "I didn't want the men to know."

Judy drew back, startled and horrified. So it was a grave he was digging and that lump in the burlap bag at his feet was all that was left of the men's spotted mascot!

"My cat killed him!" she cried.

"No, Miss Judy. It wasn't the cat. He's been sick," John explained. "He never had the life in him that a puppy should have. Don't you worry your head over it, Miss Judy. He would have died anyway."

"Oh, but that's terrible. Somebody must be to blame."

"It happens to all of us sooner or later," John said gravely.

"But what will you tell the men?" Judy asked when he turned around, his task finished.

"Don't know as there'll be any men to tell."

"My goodness! You are gloomy this morning. Why wouldn't there be?"

"The Red Circle! We heard it again just before the dog died."

"You're getting superstitious," Judy scolded. "You'll laugh at yourself some day when we find out what the Red Circle really is."

"I expect I will, Miss Judy. I hear you're good at finding out things."

"I thought I was," Judy said. "I thought I'd find out something yesterday but instead I went to sleep and so here I am, stranded in Roulsville. I was wondering if you could spare your car."

"It's an old rattlebox, but if you don't mind——"

Judy assured him she didn't. She and John had hardly started the car when the youngest of the workmen, son of the older man, drove up in an equally noisy car and shouted for them to wait.

"The Red Circle!" he yelled. "It's got Pop too. It came on him in the night and he says we're getting out of here and taking the dog with us. He sent me after the dog."

John had slowed up the car when he heard the boy calling. But now he stepped on the accelerator.

"You can't have the dog," he shouted back. "That dog was given to me."

"He was ours too-oo . . . " the boy's voice echoed back and then died in the distance. He was out of his car and stood in the road calling but John paid no attention.

"Hadn't we better go back just long enough to see what happened?" Judy suggested. "You've had three people tell you the Red Circle got them but not one of them has explained anything."

"Thought you were in a hurry to get home," John said shortly. "There's no time for explanations."

"But it may be too late," Judy protested.

"We'll hurry right back," John promised, "when your people know you're safe. I wonder your mother's hair isn't gray already."

"I often wonder that myself. But Mum's a good sport. Dad is too," Judy added. "Besides, he has so much trouble of his own on his mind that he doesn't spend much time worrying about me. He's afraid he'll lose some little girl patient in the hospital and he spends more time with her than he does with us. He feels so badly about it that I'm almost afraid to ask him how she is."

"Your father's a fine man," John agreed. "It was wonderful how he cured up my asthma. Asked me if I had goose feathers in my pillow.

Imagine! Me sleeping on goose feathers!''

"He gave you tests, I suppose?''

"He didn't need to. I had those tests made a month ago. I didn't react to anything but rice powder. There's another laugh,'' John continued. "Imagine a hard-working man like me using rice powder!''

"It's funny,'' Judy said in a puzzled voice. "Dad usually finds out a great deal from those skin tests and when a man has a sudden attack like you had there's nearly always a reason.''

"Maybe the Red Circle.''

"Now you're being funny,'' Judy said. "How could a secret society give anybody asthma?''

"So you think it's a secret society, do you?''

"I don't know what else it could be.''

"Well, I do,'' John declared. "It could be spirits. I'm not scared, mind you. I've never done anything that the dead should be haunting me—especially dead horses. I can listen to those hoof beats and keep right on hammering. But there ain't many that could do it.''

"I'm glad you can do it, John,'' Judy praised him, "because now that the old man and the boy have quit and your mascot is dead, I'm afraid you will have to finish up alone.''

CHAPTER XI

DR. BOLTON had been at the hospital all night and had just returned when Judy came home. Her mother had missed her an hour earlier when she went to call her for breakfast. She had telephoned Peter at once.

"He told me somebody told him that Arthur had brought you home so he thought he needn't drive back for you himself," she explained. "I knew there was some mistake the minute I found your bed empty. I worried so! This hour has been like a year. I rang Peter's office and there was no answer. You had already left. Come, dear, and I'll fix you some breakfast."

"I think John would like a little coffee too," Judy suggested. "He's had an unpleasant job to do this morning, digging a grave for his dog. The poor thing died after Blackberry went at him——"

"I told you, Miss Judy," John interrupted, "the dog was sick and would have died anyway."

"I hope it wasn't Blackberry's fault. The

103

bad cat! It will be a long time before I take him to Roulsville again.''

Blackberry slunk back into his corner, ashamed, as Judy put him down.

''But Peter's explanation doesn't sound like him, Mother,'' she continued. ''Didn't he get in touch with you or Arthur or anybody until you called this morning?''

''He wasn't well,'' Mrs. Bolton said, ''and I guess he was glad of a chance to stay home and rest.''

John looked up. Judy could tell from the half-interested, half-afraid look in his eyes that he was thinking of the Red Circle. How would it strike? John thought it caused his asthma. Could it possibly be the cause of Peter's illness?

''If only I knew what it was,'' Judy thought. She put down her piece of toast. John had finished his coffee and the two of them were just sitting there when, if they didn't hurry, it might be too late to ask the boy and his father anything about it.

''Let's get Peter and Horace and go back to the house at once,'' she suggested. ''While we sit here, who knows what may be going on in Roulsville?''

Before another hour had passed the rattlebox

of a car was speeding back with Horace beside
John in the front seat and Judy and Peter following in Peter's car. Peter felt quite all right now.
Horace had his notebook along and expected a
juicy bit of news when they interviewed the man
who had said the Red Circle got him.

"Where do this man and his son live?" he
asked John when they finally stopped not far
from Mrs. Piper's house and Peter and Judy
joined them.

"They're boarding at Mrs. Satterlee's Wayside Rest. It's on the main road, one of these
tourist places," John explained. "It takes
about ten minutes to drive there."

We'll follow you again," Peter agreed.
"Let's go."

Mrs. Satterlee's Wayside Rest looked anything but restful as the two cars drove in. The
woman herself, dressed in a calico dress she had
forgotten to fasten, ran down to the road.

"Sure and I've got rooms," she began before
they had had time to state their errand. "If
you'll give me a jiffy to clean them up you can
have the rooms Mr. Barker and his son just left.
You're John Olson, aren't you? He was working for you. And are these young folks the
three children?"

"Now, now, Mrs. Satterlee," John began, "you should know my three children aren't this big. These are friends of mine. They wanted to see the Barkers. But you say they've left?"

"And in such a dither what with the old man groaning and taking on and the boy sassing him back and saying what's he got to yell about. The Red Circle's got him too. What is this circle business, I should like to know?"

"So should we," Judy said. "But unless this man and boy told you where they were going it looks as though we'd never find out."

"They've left," John moaned, "just like the others. The Red Circle has spirited them away."

Horace was chuckling to himself. An unsolved mystery made better copy than one that was solved. Readers of the *Herald* would want to follow it up and find out what happened. Judy wanted to follow it up for a better reason than that. If John quit too and the house was never finished Peter would lose the money he had advanced on the loan and he would also lose all the clients who were appealing to him to help fight the Roulsville Development Company. Besides that, Mrs. Piper would lose her home.

"We'd better finish the house before anything

else happens,'' she suggested, ''and solve this mystery afterwards.''

This suited John. He was willing to work without help and without a mascot. Naturally, Judy had abandoned all thought of leaving Blackberry in Roulsville and Algie thought his chicken was safer at home too. He and his mother had lost their enthusiasm for the new house.

''I've had about all my nerves can stand,'' Mrs. Piper declared. ''One night alone in that house and I'd be ready for a padded cell. It's all right when you can explain things. Old houses get creaky stairs and rusty hinges that squeak when the doors are opened—all such things, and it's all right and natural. But when a house gets haunted before it's fairly finished and when it gets haunted, not with human ghosts, but with the ghosts of horses, that is beyond all explaining. Wasn't it a horse, Judy, that your brother rode through Roulsville when he warned people that the dam was breaking? I got to thinking about it and said to myself, 'It's that same horse come back from the spirit world——' ''

''But, Mrs. Piper,'' Judy protested, ''that horse is still alive. My grandfather owns it and

Red is still working it every day on the farm.''

"Then it's another warning. Something is going to happen and I can't stand any more. Oh, I wish I'd never seen the house!" Mrs. Piper cried. "Nothing but trouble! Trouble! Trouble! Is there no end to it? What will my poor little boy do?"

She was growing hysterical again. Judy couldn't talk to her when she went on like that. But she could sympathize and her determination to solve the mystery of the Red Circle and those uncanny horses grew by the minute. The following morning she rode to Roulsville again with Peter and they both stopped off at the house to see how the work was progressing and if any more had been learned about the mysteries surrounding it.

The house had windows now. But the narrow plank was still the only means of entering it. The plaster was on the walls but the woodwork was not yet painted and there were little round holes in the plaster with electric wires coming through. These were where the light fixtures would be placed when the house was finished.

"John ought to be through in another day or two," Judy remarked as she followed Peter along the plank.

"It's awfully quiet," he said. "Do you suppose he has quit too?"

"He wouldn't!" gasped Judy.

But, as they walked on through the empty house, both of them began to think he would. If the Red Circle had struck the workmen, might it not strike John too?

They did not say this to each other. But every footstep of theirs, ringing through the rooms, said it in hollow echoes. Suddenly Judy spoke.

"Perhaps those horses people thought they heard were only the echoes we hear now."

"But all empty houses are like this," Peter objected. "Nobody would mistake the echo of a human footstep for the clattering of horses' hoofs on a race track. And you do remember that John thought, at first, there was a race track near by?"

"Yes," Judy answered thoughtfully. "I remember."

"What'll we do if we can't find John?"

"Go to his house," Judy suggested.

"And suppose he's not there?"

"We'll cross that bridge when we come to it. John's no quitter."

So, after searching through the unfinished house and finding no trace of him, Judy and

Peter walked on toward the other house where John Olsen lived with his wife and three children. They were nearly there when they observed John himself coming toward them.

"On my way to work," he explained, trying to hide a bandaged arm behind him.

"What happened to you?" Judy asked. "You've hurt your arm."

"It's nothing," John said shortly. "Little pimple. Thought I'd better tie it up."

Judy looked at his grim face and then down at his arm that was stiff with bandages.

"It looks like more than a pimple to me," she said. "I hope it's nothing dangerous. None of us would want you to be injured."

"Forget it." And again John repeated, "I'm no quitter."

It was easy to say "Forget it" but when John appeared the following day with an additional bandage on his head Judy refused to pass it off as lightly as she had done before.

"You've been attacked by something," she declared, "and if it's this mysterious Red Circle we've all been wondering about, I wish you'd tell us everything that happened."

"But nothing happened," John insisted. "It just come on me in the night like this. It was the Red Circle all right. But it works—silent and in the dark.''

He paused before making this last impressive statement and Judy almost held her breath.

"But tell me,'' Judy implored. "What happens when the Red Circle strikes?''

"It just strikes,'' John said. "It leaves its mark! But I ain't quitting until this house is done.''

"Any more bandages,'' Judy told him, "and you quit whether the work is finished or not. There's no need of a man's risking his life to earn a few extra dollars. I guess, if it comes to that, Mrs. Piper can live in her house without the steps. If we can walk in along a plank, so can she.''

"You won't let the poor woman move in with those horses——''

"No, John. We'll move the horses out first. Leave it to us. And remember, no more bandages.''

CHAPTER XII

Judy went to Roulsville every day now. She was helping Peter in his law office. "Acting as his secretary," she proudly told her friends.

Peter had a great many new clients. People who heard of his attempt to expose the real estate racket came to him freely for advice. Nearly all of them hung onto the land they had won, refusing to buy the adjoining property.

"If Mrs. Piper can build a house on fifteen feet of land, we can too," they told each other.

They kept Judy busy answering letters, answering the telephone and keeping Peter's files in order. A grocery box served as a filing cabinet as Peter was not so much interested in making money out of his new clients as he was in making a reputation for honesty and fair dealing. It would mean more to him to be known as the lawyer who beat the real estate racket than to be called "that rich Mr. Dobbs."

Mrs. Piper's house was an experiment that

interested Peter and his clients almost as much
as it interested Judy. So, no matter how busy
they were, either Judy or Peter or both of them
together found time to run down some time during the day and see how John was getting along
with the work.

The day after John appeared with the bandages on his head, they started for Roulsville a
little earlier than usual. A great deal of work
was waiting for them in the office and they
hoped to start in on it as soon as they made sure
nothing more had happened to John.

"If only he finishes," Judy said, "and Mrs.
Piper isn't afraid to move in, then our biggest
battle will be won."

"We can't win while the Red Circle is making
threats and apparently carrying them out,"
Peter declared.

"But we can beat the Red Circle, just like
you're beating the Real Estate Racket," Judy
said with confidence. But she added, in a somewhat less confident tone, "I wish it weren't
quite such a gloomy day. Things aren't so apt
to go wrong when the sun is shining."

So far the sun had kept himself well hidden.
Even before they started Judy had noticed that
the sky was gray with only a slight yellowish

tint in the east. She thought at first that it was only a little misty because it was so early in the morning. But, as they drove on toward Roulsville, the grayness began to settle over them. It was growing darker by the minute. Peter glanced up at the gathering clouds.

"It looks like a storm."

"That will delay work worse than anything," mourned Judy. "Everything's finished but the porch and the front steps and John can't work outside in the rain. Dad says a thorough chilling might bring a sudden attack of pneumonia. You know how he suffers from asthma already."

"And with those bandages——"

Judy shuddered. "We mustn't let him work, Peter. He's afraid of thunder storms. I remember how he said those horses reminded him of thunder."

"Maybe that's what the horses were."

"Oh, no. You remember, it was a clear day. I wouldn't mind hearing the horses. It would be a mystery to solve and I'd be too curious to be frightened. But I am afraid of thunder," Judy confided, snuggling a little closer to Peter as he drove the car.

"I can't say as I blame you," Peter sympathized. "I'm not so keen on thunder storms myself, especially in Roulsville."

"I guess they remind us both of the big storm when the dam broke and we lost our homes," Judy said sadly.

She sat that way for a minute, looking downcast and unhappy and then looked up with a strange suggestion.

"Peter," she said, "we both hate storms. Why do we have to ride right into one? Why can't we turn back?"

"Turn back!" he exclaimed. "Is this my big, brave Judy—turning back because it's going to rain? And after facing all the dangers you've faced? What's come over you, girl? Judy doesn't do those things."

"I guess she doesn't," Judy admitted, a little ashamed. "But all of us have our fears and a storm is mine, especially a freak storm." She shivered. "Gracious, it's cold. I wish I'd brought an extra wrap."

"It is growing colder," Peter agreed. "And look how queer the sky is! You'd almost think this was a snow storm coming up. The sky is gray enough for a snow storm. But we don't have snow in May."

"Don't we?" Judy held out her hand. "Look, Peter! That's a snowflake on my glove now. Oh, goody! I'm glad it's snow instead of thunder and lightning. I'm not afraid of snow."

It was snowing in earnest now, big, fluffy flakes like pieces of frosting descending on some enormous cake. It blew against the windshield and ridged the road with white.

"This is thrilling!" Judy cried. "We'll have snow right on top of our spring flowers. But I suppose it will kill them," she added more seriously. "I guess I don't like freak weather any more than I thought I did."

"John can't work in the snow any better than he can in the rain."

"I hadn't thought of that. Oh, Peter! Everything's against us, even the weather. You'd almost think the real estate people did this on purpose."

"You can blame the mysterious order of the Red Circle on them if you want to," Peter said, "but hardly the weather. We'll park the car here." He drew up next to the curb. Across the street was Mrs. Piper's house and in the yard were what, at first, looked like tracks in the snow.

"John's there!" Judy exclaimed, jumping out of the car. "There are his tracks . . . But Peter! Are they tracks?"

She ran ahead a few feet and then drew back in horror. Not a track was on the even surface of the new-fallen snow. What looked like tracks from a distance now appeared round and red and terrible.

"The Red Circle! But Peter, there are no tracks! How could a person leave such a warning and not leave tracks as well?"

"Search me! Gosh! This is the worst yet."

The circles were exactly like those first nail marks—not even circles of red, but dots like drops of blood on the snow. Sometimes there was but one circle. Sometimes there was one within another. And they were all over the yard. What could it mean?

"John!" Judy shouted. "John!"

Only an echo answered from the empty house.

"Those echoes are frightful," she said. "I'd rather hear the horses."

"You will," Peter prophesied, "if we stay here much longer. We may be wearing bandages on our heads too. Come, Judy! We must find out what's happened to John. Let's go to his home."

Peter had difficulty starting the car because of the sudden cold. But finally the motor coughed and began to throb. The old bus churned through the streets of Roulsville, past peach trees heavy with peach blossoms and snow. Snow lined the little tree branches that were just sprouting leaves. It was weird, this snow storm. It put the hush of a graveyard over the whole town. John's house, like all the others, was quiet under its mantle of snow.

Peter rung the bell and John's wife, a gaunt woman with a powerful personality, came to the door.

"John's sleeping," she said with a broad, Swedish accent. "He's not to be disturbed."

"But this is important—" Judy began.

"He's not to be disturbed," the woman shouted. "He's done with the house and done with you and he's not to be disturbed!"

That appeared to be that. For a moment Judy could think of nothing more to say. It was like talking back to a volcano. But finally she found her voice.

"Is your husband ill?"

"When he's ill he'll send for the doctor!"

"This is his doctor," Judy said meekly, handing Mrs. Olsen her father's card. She turned to Peter and together they walked down the steps, their shoes creaking in the snow as they walked.

"It's no use," Judy said when they were in the car again. "Our only hope is that he sends for Dad."

"But what are we going to do about the house?" Peter asked.

"What is there to do," Judy replied, "but tackle the problem ourselves? John's done. The house is as nearly finished as it will be for a long time. So, as soon as the ghosts move out, I see no reason why Mrs. Piper can't move in."

"And how, little Miss Detective, are we to set about moving the ghosts?"

"Find out what they are," Judy replied, "and then, like all other ghosts, they will vanish into the air—or into the police station," she added, remembering another house she had "de-haunted" as Peter called it.

"And I suppose I'll be called upon to help, as usual? And I suppose you have plans for finding out these ghosts?"

"Yes, I do have plans," Judy stated. "The simplest plans in the world. How do most people find out what haunts a house? Why, by

staying there over night! And that's exactly
what I mean to do. "

"Judy! Not alone?"

"Well, no," Judy admitted. "I hadn't
thought of staying there all alone. Maybe Mrs.
Piper will stay with me. And maybe you and
Horace could sleep in the office and we could
arrange some sort of signal in case I'm in danger. Do you think we could?"

"It sounds reasonable. But I'm afraid for
you, Judy."

"You needn't be afraid," Judy told him. "I
won't be afraid if I know you're nearby to help.
It's the only way to solve the mystery."

CHAPTER XIII

THE MYSTERIOUS BLUE FLAME

JUDY had it all planned before the day had passed. On the way home she told Peter.

"We'll get Mrs. Piper's permission and take over some blankets and bedding and maybe a bridge table and folding chairs and some dishes in case we want to eat——"

"In case!" laughed Peter. "I never yet met a girl who didn't want to eat."

"Oh, all right! We'll take a lot of things then. Mrs. Piper will be glad of anything we bring and Mother has several pieces of furniture she doesn't need. It's going to be fun."

"That's what you always say."

"And it always is fun too. You know it is, Peter, when you and I do things like this together. We'll have everything moved in tomorrow and I'll fix it up and we can stay in Roulsville tomorrow night—Mrs. Piper and me at the house and you and Horace at the office."

"Tomorrow night? That's Friday, isn't it?" Peter said thoughtfully.

Judy had been so interested she had forgotten about his Fridays. The garden party was on Friday and he couldn't come. It was a Friday night he had failed to come for her and left her to sleep in his office.

"It's Friday," Judy reasoned, "that he has his date with Miss Ames."

She set her lips together. How long was this silly affair going to last? And why must she put up with it?

"Call up Miss Ames," she said suddenly, "and break your appointment. This mystery is more important."

"Do you really think it is, Judy?"

Why was he so serious, acting as if she had broken through into something sacred? In some way, she had hurt him. But she couldn't imagine how.

Silently, Judy told herself she must have faith until everything was explained. But she couldn't ask Peter for an explanation now. If she spoke again she would cry and it would look so silly to cry over a boy right to his face. So, when he stopped the car, she waited until she was on the porch and the temptation to tears was gone. Then she turned and called. "All right, Peter! It's Saturday."

But she couldn't get the thought out of her mind. "His date with Miss Ames is more important than the mystery or me or anything."

The thought was still in Judy's mind when she went to ask Mrs. Piper's permission to stay in the house and the woman suggested Friday.

"I don't think I'd mind staying there one night," she said, leaning across her bare kitchen table as she talked to Judy. "It would take my mind off things and anything would be better than sitting in this bare room worrying my heart out. And I did want to get the house fixed up and ready before Dow comes home."

Dow was her husband. She spoke of him as Dow just as she called Judy by her given name now that they were more friendly.

"You know," she went on in a confidential tone, "I think he might get to care about me again if I had a nice home fixed up for him and he could bring in his friends instead of taking them out to a bar. He's a fine man, Judy. It's just the way he takes trouble. He has to drink to forget it."

"It's a selfish way to take it," Judy said, "especially when he's the cause of the trouble."

"But he isn't!" Mrs. Piper gasped. "Whatever made you think that?"

"Well, if he worked—and you had things——"

"There are some things," Mrs. Piper interrupted, "that no amount of money could buy. It's the way life is and you just have to learn to smile through it and make the best of it."

"He could help—if he wasn't so selfish," Judy said. "But I guess all men are like that. Even Peter. He has a date with some girl Friday night so we have to wait 'til Saturday."

"Oh, but I wanted to get away on Friday night! I have to! Couldn't you and I stay there alone?"

Judy knew she should have said that was impossible. But Mrs. Piper was so insistent. And she hated to admit that she was a little afraid of the house herself unless Peter was somewhere near to help her. Those signals they had planned! Why, they would all be useless if Peter wasn't at his office. One candle burning in the window was to signify that they heard the ghosts but were in no danger. Two candles would mean slight danger. Be ready to help. And three candles, DANGER! Come at once!

"Couldn't we make it Friday?" Mrs. Piper repeated.

"Yes," Judy agreed, "I suppose we could.

I imagine everything would be quiet at night anyway. Those noises were probably meant to frighten the workmen away and nobody would bother us.''

But what about the red circles in the snow? Another, more sensible Judy seemed to be asking Judy the question. There was something to be afraid of. She needed Peter to help. But if Peter thought another girl was more important . . . And there it was, all over again. The eternal question in her mind. Why must Peter see Miss Ames every Friday night?

"I'll get Algie to sleep early," Mrs. Piper went on. "He will have his chicken. So don't take your cat, Judy. It's apt to cause trouble.''

She couldn't have Blackberry either! This staying in the unfinished house on Friday seemed more and more senseless. But, somehow, it was agreed. Mrs. Bolton consented to the plan more readily than she would have done if Mrs. Piper hadn't been going to stay in the house too. Judy had told her there were some spooky noises she wanted to investigate. But she hadn't said there was any real danger. She didn't really think there was. Nevertheless, she was afraid. Nothing was sure any more. Mrs. Piper's house was haunted with more than

ghost horses. It was haunted with fear. Judy
was trembling when, at last, she walked up the
plank and across the skeleton-like framework
of the porch and into the empty rooms.

"You're not afraid, are you?" Mrs. Piper
asked anxiously.

"It's cold enough to make anyone shivery
after that snow," Judy said. "Suppose we
light a fire and try to make it cozy. Then we
can fix something to eat and put Algie to bed
and—wait."

But she paused a little too long before she
said, "wait." It left a question in Mrs. Piper's
mind. "Wait for what?"

"Did they take away the horses?" Algie
asked suddenly.

"They will," Judy assured him, trying to
make her voice sound confident.

"Can I see them this time?" Algie persisted.
"I don't like horses I can't see."

"Neither do I," Judy agreed. "But if the
horses play hide-and-seek with us tonight, I'll
be 'it' and find them."

"Can I hunt too?"

"We'll see. But first we're going to set the
chairs all nice around the table and fix these
pretty cushions your mother made and spread

this nice cover on the cot and then we'll have our first dinner in the new house. Won't that be fun?''

"But I want to play hide-and-seek with the horses. I want to pla-ay——"

"You see," Judy said, interrupting what was beginning to be a tantrum, "now he's going to cry because the house isn't haunted."

They both laughed at that and Algie calmed down and began helping. In almost no time the empty rooms were beginning to look more cheerful with the gay cushions scattered about and the furniture tastefully arranged in the various nooks and corners. Some Spring flowers, cut just before the snow storm, were still fresh enough to look pretty in a blue vase on the table.

"Now all we need to make it homelike is a nice warm fire. There's some rubbish the workmen left in the kitchen and we might as well burn that," Mrs. Piper suggested.

The rubbish consisted of brown paper bags with scraps from past lunches in them, excelsior, sawed-off ends of wood and little curly-cues of shavings stuffed into a broken peach basket. Judy piled it, peach basket and all, into the fireplace. Then she struck a match.

"What is it the campfire girls say over their fires?" she asked.

"Burn, fire! Burn!
Flicker, flicker, flame!
Whose hand above this blaze is lifted
Shall be with magic touch ingifted . . . "

"Judy!" Mrs. Piper cried. "Will you look at your fire? I never saw anything like it in my life. It's almost as if it was magic. Look, Judy! the flame is blue—and those red circles!"

Judy started back from the fire and stared. It was burning brightly now. She could see the blue flame all right. But the red circles had disappeared.

"Maybe it was only the wire from the peach basket," Judy suggested.

"But that wasn't it," Mrs. Piper protested. "They were small circles. They burned red for a minute and then went up in blue flame."

Red circles again! How glad Judy was that Mrs. Piper knew nothing of their sinister meaning. First the snow and now the fire had warned her. Tonight she would surely hear the horses. And tonight—she shivered to think of it—she and Mrs. Piper and Algie would be alone.

CHAPTER XIV

THE HOUSE IS HAUNTED

"I've been wanting to talk with you for quite a while," Mrs. Piper said, moving closer to Judy as they sat before the fire. "You see, I feel that you're my friend."

"I guess I must be," Judy answered apprehensively, "or I wouldn't be here. I don't like the looks of things at all."

"I don't either—or I didn't," Mrs. Piper amended, "until you promised to stay with me. Now I'm not afraid. I've heard such things about you, Judy, you can't imagine. Even the chief of police says there isn't a girl in Farringdon who can hold a candle to you for courage. I met him the other day and asked his advice and he said just to leave everything to you. You were the only professional ghost chaser he knew."

Judy laughed in spite of her fears. It was a big reputation to live up to and tonight she felt far from courageous.

"A ghost chaser, am I? And everything ghostly white outside and me as cold as a ghost —or aren't ghosts cold? They must be," Judy reflected, "or they wouldn't make people shiver. I'm shivery now. Let's stir up the fire."

"I'll do it," Mrs. Piper offered.

Judy watched her as she thrust the poker underneath the rubbish and piled on more wood. But this time there were no red circles and the flame was only slightly blue.

If she could explain the red circles in some logical way, Judy knew they would cease to be so frightening. She felt almost sure that, once she heard them, she could explain the horses.

"I do hope something happens tonight— something that I can investigate," she said. "It would be a fine time for your ghost horses to race—on a snowy track."

"Ghost horses? Don't speak of them," Mrs. Piper replied with a shudder. "They were frightful. I thought at first I'd never come back to this house. But it wasn't so much because I couldn't see the horses. I remembered the Roulsville flood and it seemed like another warning. I was sure something had happened to Clara."

"Your little girl?   The one that's away visiting——''

"That's what I want Algie and his father to think,'' Mrs. Piper said in a lower voice. She almost whispered although there was little danger of waking Algie. He had fallen asleep after Judy had read him three chapters from his favorite Oz book and was now peacefully dreaming of the scarecrow or the tin woodman or, perhaps, the funny patchwork girl. Judy had carried him to his own room just above the living room and no word of the conversation downstairs could reach his ears.

"I don't understand,'' Judy said, her voice also hushed. "You mean you wanted Algie and Mr. Piper to think something that wasn't true?''

"Oh, Judy! You put it so bluntly.''

"Perhaps I do,'' Judy replied, "but I've always been taught that the truth, no matter how unpleasant, is always best.''

"Do you really think it is? I mean when Algie and his father are so nervous and all— when they can't stand it to be frightened—and when—and when——''

She hesitated. She was trying to tell Judy something that was difficult to put in words.

Judy settled her back against the brick of the fireplace, prepared to listen. "I'll try not to be priggish," she promised. "Dad tells me I judge people too quickly. I mustn't judge you, I know. If you told Algie his sister was visiting in the country when she was really somewhere else I'm sure you had a good reason."

"I thought I had. But everything is so mixed up. I find myself telling him more and more things that aren't true in order to cover up what I told him at first."

"That's the way it is. I think it was Shakespeare who said something about a tangled web——"

Mrs. Piper huddled up her knees and stared into the fire.

"Don't talk of spiders," she said. "It's spooky enough in here without talking of spiders—and ghosts."

Judy glanced about at the long shadows the flickering fire threw on the opposite wall. It was spooky.

"I didn't mean to speak of anything unpleasant," she said. "I was talking about the difficulties people get into—not spiders. I was just comparing them."

"Don't compare things, Judy. I'll be doing

it too. That wind outside is like—is like——"

"Is like the rustle of silk," Judy finished, "and quite a nice comparison too."

"But I wasn't going to say that," Mrs. Piper objected. "It isn't like the rustle of silk. It's like something moaning. Hear it!"

It did sound too human for the wind. But Judy tried to keep Mrs. Piper from listening.

"You were telling me something," she began.

"It whistles too!" Mrs. Piper cried. "Hear it! Judy, are you sure it is the wind?"

"I'll go upstairs and see," Judy replied, rising quickly and running up the bare stairs with such haste that whatever the noise was it could not be heard above the clatter of her shoes. When she was at the top she stood still and for a moment her errand seemed absurd. How could anybody run upstairs and see if the wind was whistling? If it whistled, then it would naturally whistle all over the house. It wouldn't be any louder in one place than it was in another.

Judy listened a moment. Either her logic was wrong or this thing that was whistling was very close at hand. The whistling was much louder on the second floor. It would wake Algie!

The little boy turned restlessly in his bed, sighed, and was then sound asleep again.

"Thank Heaven!" Judy thought. "If he ever wakes up and hears this he'll know it isn't the wind."

There was a certain cadence to the noise. It wouldn't have been unpleasant if Judy knew where it came from. Perhaps a neighbor's radio. But there were no neighbors.

"Well," she told herself. "I expected something like this. So did Mrs. Piper."

They'd face it. That was all there was to do. No use saying, "Maybe it's a radio. Maybe it's the wind." No use fooling themselves.

"I didn't find out what the noise was," Judy stated simply when she returned to the living room. "But I found out what it wasn't. It whistled sort of a tune and so it couldn't have been the wind."

Mrs. Piper's eyes widened and her hand clutched the neck of her dress.

"We're not going to lose our heads about this and run around like a couple of frightened chickens," Judy went on determinedly. "You were telling me yourself just a minute ago how mixed up everything gets if you try to cover things up. So let's not. Let's not cover up the

fact that we both know this house is supposed
to be haunted——"

"Haunted? You mean *ghosts?*"

"I don't mean anything supernatural," Judy
said. "But the workmen heard this same
whistling and were unable to explain it. Now
if we can keep our chins up and not be afraid,
we may do better."

"I'll try," Mrs. Piper promised. "There
are worse things than haunted houses."

"Of course," Judy agreed. "Haunted
houses are fun after the scare is over. Think
of all we'll have to talk about!"

Upstairs Algie woke up and screamed.

"It's the wind," his mother told him, lifting
him out of bed. "Come down by the fire with
us and we'll sing real loud and not hear it."

Down by the fire all three of them sang with
more noise than tune. They tried to sing above
the whistling but now it had risen to almost
a screech. Algie had stopped singing and was
now drowning out the whistling noise with
screams.

"You shouldn't have told him it was the
wind," Judy said, taking the screaming child
away from his mother. "He knows it isn't."

Algie gulped. "Wh-what is it then?"

"We don't know, dear," Judy replied. "But if you'll stop crying and help us, we may find out."

"I wouldn't want to find out a gho-ost."

"I would," Judy said, her voice very brave. "I'd like to find one out and slap him on the back and watch him vanish."

Algie giggled, a hysterical little giggle that was half a sob.

"You're funny," he said.

Judy didn't feel very funny. But pretending helped. Peter always pretended frightening things were funny and, most usually, it turned out that Peter was right.

"You know, if I were a little boy like you," Judy said, "I think I'd like being in a haunted house. I told you we were going to play hide-and-seek with the horses. But the horses haven't come yet so now we're playing with these funny noises. They're hiding and we're supposed to find them."

"I'll look upstairs then," Algie said firmly. "They're louder upstairs."

Ten minutes passed and the whistling died down. Judy tiptoed upstairs and found Algie fast asleep on the floor beside his bed. She laughed softly.

"I guess he was looking under the bed for the noises."

"It was wonderful how you told him," Mrs. Piper praised Judy as they walked back downstairs. "If I'd told him anything about ghosts it would have scared him half to death."

"Perhaps it's the way you tell him. When he sees you're trying to hide something that makes him afraid."

"Maybe. I was going to talk about it but now that everything's quiet again I guess we'd better go to bed."

Judy would have preferred to stay up. But she couldn't deny that Mrs. Piper's suggestion was a sensible one. They were both tired and needed the sleep. There was a bed ready for Mrs. Piper upstairs in the room with Algie and Judy could sleep on the cot in the living room. She was glad she had brought her warm pajamas because the room was chilly now that the fire was dying and there was only one extra blanket. Judy pulled it up to her neck, trying to make herself comfortable, but every nerve in her body was tense. A dozen questions crowded into her mind. Was it safe down here alone? Were Mrs. Piper and Algie safe upstairs? Would it be better if all three of them were together? But no, that would leave the upstairs room empty in case anyone attempted to enter the house. Foolish fears! They seemed still more foolish as the night wore on and nothing happened.

But Judy lay awake expecting something to happen and listening to all the small night noises, exaggerated through the stillness, until even the faint ticking of her watch became enormous in the dark. She struck a match and saw that in ten more minutes it would be midnight. Still nothing happened.

Judy's bed was near the window. She could see the wet pane where the late snow was mixing with a fine rain which would melt it by morning unless it grew colder soon. She didn't want the snow to melt. If anybody came, the tracks in the snow might provide a clue. But if there were no tracks? She remembered that there had been none where the red circles were and again she wondered how anyone could mark red circles in the snow without leaving tracks beside them. The thought grew large and frightening. Even though the red circles in the yard were now melted away, Judy seemed to see them dancing behind her closed eyelids. How could she sleep? How could anybody sleep when, at any moment, the red circle might strike?

That was what John had said. "Nothing happened. It just came on me in the night. The Red Circle works silent and in the dark!" Well, nothing was happening now—nothing at all. And yet, when she awoke . . .

"That's just it," Judy thought, "if I don't go to sleep I can't wake up and find that something terrible has happened."

She sat up in bed. She wouldn't let herself sleep. There were Mrs. Piper and Algie to be considered. Every so often she must tiptoe into their room and make sure they were all right. She lit one of the candles she had planned to flash across the darkness as a signal to Peter. The house was unfinished and so there were no lights in it except the light of candles. How peacefully Mrs. Piper and Algie were sleeping! How they must trust her! And yet how frightened and how alone she felt with nobody to help her!

Judy lay down again and then got up once more to place her candle in the window. It would be comforting to light it even if Peter couldn't see it. She wished, at least, she had asked Horace to come along. He would be some

comfort even though he was a scairdy-cat himself, at times. She laughed, remembering how
his face looked like a full moon when he was
frightened. She imaged how it would look if
he heard the ghost horses. Ghost horses at
midnight! How weird and exicting and strange
it would be if Judy heard them now—*Clop!*
Clop! Clop!—coming down some ghostly race
track. *Clop! Clop! Clop!*

Was it raining on top of the snow? Big
drops? They'd have to be as big as horses to
make a sound like that.

Clop! Clop! Clop!

Judy was out of bed again, striking a match
and lighting her candle, while the invisible
hoofs of the ghost horses trotted faster—faster.
Her heart raced with them. Upstairs! Downstairs! She did not know where to turn.
Algie's wails echoed through the house and
Judy started for the stairs but, before she had
taken two steps, a sharp rap sounded on the
door.

It was repeated—*knock! knock! knock!*

"Don't answer it!" Mrs. Piper screamed
down the bannisters. "I'll look out from the
dormer window and tell you who—*or what*—is
there."

CHAPTER XV

AFTER the first sharp knocking, there followed a moment of silence. Even the horses' hoofs were silent. Judy, oddly enough, thought of a poem she knew. It was called "The Listeners" and the listeners were the phantoms inside an empty house.

"I feel like one of them," Judy thought, "standing here, quietly, while some one outside is trying to get in."

The traveler, it was in the poem. He came on his horse and knocked on the door of the empty house and called, "Is anybody there?"

"But only a host of phantom listeners
    That dwelt in the lone house then
    Stood listening in the quiet of the moonlight
    To that voice from the world of men."

"It's a man!" Mrs. Piper called in a loud whisper. "He's standing on the porch but I can't see who he is. Don't answer the door!"

141

"But Mrs. Piper——"

"Don't answer the door!"

This time her whisper was a clear command. The traveler would go away and Judy would never know who had come to their door at midnight—or why. That was worse than fear—not knowing. That was what made Algie scream and throw himself into tantrums. Judy herself felt that she would like to scream out a protest. But the house was Mrs. Piper's house and if Mrs. Piper said not to open the door Judy knew she must not open it. It was a plain varnished door with no glass in it—only a brass knocker. This kind of door had been chosen because it was most attractive. It proved to be only one of a number of mistakes in the construction of the house. Judy could not even look out to see who was knocking unless she looked, as Mrs. Piper was looking, from the dormer window.

"Is anybody there?"

The traveler! But he was calling with Peter's voice.

"It's Peter!" Judy cried. "Oh, Mrs. Piper! It's Peter and he's come to help us and we almost didn't let him in."

Peter knocked again.

"For he suddenly smote on the door, even
Louder, and lifted his head:
'Tell them I came and nobody answered,
That I kept my word,' he said."

Like the traveler in the famous poem, Peter
had kept his word. But Judy had broken hers.
She flung open the door and sobbed on his
shoulder, "Oh, Peter! Forgive me. I should
have waited until Saturday the way you asked
me to."

"It's all right, Judy girl. I came as soon as
I could."

"And we almost didn't let you in. Poor
traveler! But you didn't come on a horse,
did you, Peter?"

"No, I came in a car as far as the office.
Horace came with me—and brought Blackberry. The poor cat looked lonesome. They'll
be here in a minute. I started running when I
saw your light."

"I don't know why I lit it."

"Wasn't something happening to make you
afraid?"

"The horses," Judy said. "But I didn't
think the candle would be any use because you
wouldn't be there to see it."

Down the street, Judy could see Horace coming slowly, carrying the cat. He wasn't hurrying. And, every so often, he would stop and stroke Blackberry. Finally, when he reached the house and began walking along the plank onto the skeleton of the porch, he said:

"Here's your black baby, Judy. He's either homesick or just plain sick. I can't tell which."

"Thank you, Horace," Judy answered, taking the cat. "But Mrs. Piper asked me not to bring him. She won't like it."

"Take a chance and put him down on one of her cushions," Peter suggested. "He looks sleepy."

So Judy lay Blackberry on a cushion where he stretched himself and closed his eyes.

Upstairs, Algie had stopped sobbing to ask who the men were and Judy could hear Mrs. Piper patiently explaining that they were just two big boys who had come to help hunt for horses. That was better. She was telling him the truth now and he seemed to be quieting down again. Judy explained things to Peter and Horace. She told them how they had heard all the ghostly noises the workmen had heard and how, so far, there wasn't a clue.

"I can't think where they're coming from,"

she went on in a puzzled voice. "There aren't any secret rooms in this house and even if there were I'd like to know how anybody could get horses into them."

"Maybe they aren't horses," Peter suggested. "Maybe they're reindeer and we're having Christmas in May instead of December."

"And maybe Santa Claus is driving them over the roof," Horace finished with a grin.

"Well, maybe," laughed Judy. "But it isn't very likely. Come on in and we'll sit here quietly and maybe we'll hear them again and you can figure them out."

The boys came on into the living room. Peter seemed only too glad to sit quietly. He looked especially pale and tired tonight.

"He shouldn't have a date at all, with all the work he's doing," Judy thought. "Miss Ames shouldn't . . . But I'm the one who's keeping him up. If I'd only waited, the way he asked me to."

They were sitting before the fireplace, each one thinking his own thoughts and nobody saying a word when, suddenly, the silence was broken by a low, whistling noise like a long-drawn sigh.

Blackberry, on his borrowed cushion, twitched

one ear and looked up with a sleepy, half-interest. Peter sat straight in his chair and Horace lifted his hand.

"Listen!"

All at once the air vibrated with the thud of horses' hoofs.

Clop! Clop! Clop!

Again the ghost horses were racing. The traveler was here, safe before the fire. It was the horses who were the phantoms. The listeners were real.

"I'm not a bit afraid with you boys here," Judy spoke up. "It will be thrilling just to say we have heard them. First the horses racing and then—silence. Can't you almost feel it? Remember how it says in the poem:

"And the silence surged softly backward
    When the plunging hoofs were gone"?

"So that's what you meant when you called me 'poor traveler'," Peter said. "I begin to see the connection."

"And you kept your word."

"Yes," he agreed, "I managed to keep my word and keep both appointments. It looks as if the little girl is going to pull through and

Judy, I swear, I'll be tempted to call it all off and find a girl with a heart if you say you aren't glad.''

"He's right," Horace put it, "a fellow like Peter's too good for a girl who holds a promise above everything.''

"A promise?''

"He promised to come to the garden party and you expected him to be there, didn't you?''

"Oh, yes! Yes!" Judy cried. "But please don't ask me any more riddles until we've solved a few . . . WE HAVE . . . ALREADY! Goodness! I do have to shout above those horses. What's that? Algie screaming again?''

"I don't b'lieve you! I don't b'lieve you!" the little boy's voice rose louder and louder.

"You stay down here and keep your eyes open, Horace. Come," Judy motioned Peter. "You and I will go upstairs.''

This was a real tantrum. Algie, wide-eyed and frightened, had the bed to himself and lay there kicking and screaming.

"I don't believe you! It's not boys! It's MEN! It's DOCTORS—and they took Daddy away and they took Clara away and now they're going to take me-ee!''

"But Daddy's at Grandma's—" Mrs. Piper tried to explain.

"He isn't! He isn't! And Clara isn't at Auntie's! The doctor's got them both and THOSE ARE DOCTORS' HORSES!"

"Listen to him!" Judy laughed. "A doctor's horses! Why, Algie! I should think a big boy like you ought to know that doctors don't drive horses any more. They have their own cars."

"D-do they?"

He swallowed a scream and looked straight at Judy. Then he saw Peter and pointed.

"Is he a doctor?"

"No, dear. He's a lawyer. He's come to help hunt for horses, the way your mother said."

"But Mommie told me Clara was at my auntie's and I saw my auntie and she said——"

"Hush, dear!"

"Let him go on," Judy pleaded. "Something is troubling him and he wants to explain."

"—And she said Clara wasn't there," he finished with a sob.

"Perhaps you'd better tell him where his sister really is," Peter suggested.

"I can't! I c-can't! Oh, can't you see I

can't tell him? He couldn't hear me anyway
ABOVE THOSE HORSES!''

Clop! Clop! Clop! Louder and louder
sounded the thundering hoofs. The house itself seemed to tremble.

*Clop! Clop! Clop! They're coming down
the home stretch! Red Circle is ahead! He's
going to strike tonight—and tomorrow—and the
next day—and the next day——*

''That voice gives him away,'' Judy said.
''It's the limerick singer. Remember, the other
day when Mrs. Piper and Algie heard the
horses, we saw him racing toward Roulsville in
his car. Remember, Peter?''

''I remember,'' Peter said grimly. ''So you
think this is a show put on with the intention of
scaring us half out of our wits?''

''Yes, but I refuse to be scared.''

''So do I—because——'' Peter paused im-
pressively. ''Because that voice doesn't happen to be the limerick singer at all. It's the
voice of a famous radio announcer and this
show is simply a program on somebody's
radio.''

''But Peter, it couldn't be that,'' Judy
shouted above the racing horses. ''You can

feel the house shake when those horses begin trotting. And who would broadcast such a program—on purpose to scare us—and mention the Red Circle?"

"The Red Circle!" gasped Mrs. Piper. "Isn't Red Circle just the name of a horse?"

"I can find out in a minute," Peter promised. "There's a radio set in my office. I'll go over and tune it in. Keep Horace on the job and remember the signals while I'm gone!"

"I'll remember. But Peter, if it is only a radio I wish you'd take a candle and flash a signal too."

Judy watched for the signal through the dormer window while Horace kept a lookout downstairs. But no signal came. The horses hoofs beat louder and louder. Horace left his post for a minute and stood at the head of the stairs.

"You were right, Judy," he said. "That's no radio. It's somebody hiding on the roof. I'm going out and see who it is."

"Wait, Horace! I'll go with you."

They turned, startled by the look of panic in Mrs. Piper's eyes.

"Oh, please," she begged. "One of you must stay with me."

CHAPTER XVI

"I'LL stay," Judy volunteered, "but hurry, Horace! You can't imagine how curious I am."

"Can't I, though!" Affecting a Scotch accent, he added, "I'm a wee bit curious meself."

And, with a flourish of the reporter's notebook he always carried, he was gone. But no sooner had he closed the door than something else was heard to bang and the beating of the horses' hoofs suddenly ceased.

Silence! Dead silence! Had Horace actually scared some prowler off the roof? Was the mystery solved so easily? But of course it wasn't. One man on the roof of one little house would never solve the mystery of a dozen racing horses.

Through the silence that followed the sudden cessation of the strange noises they had been hearing, Judy's ears detected a faint crackling like the snapping of a dry twig or—

"Or," she thought in alarm, "a pine needle

151

crackling in a bonfire.'' At the same time she caught a whiff of something. A burned match? That's what it smelled like. But Judy knew the truth. Somewhere in the house there was a fire! And it wasn't in the fireplace either for the sound she had heard was distinctly over her head. She turned to Mrs. Piper and said, through white lips, ''We must get Algie out of here quickly. I think there's a fire on the roof.''

''A fire?''

''Be careful. Don't alarm him. If he's old enough to go to school then he realizes that children march out for fire drills in an orderly line. We'll march out now. Come, Algie! One. Two. Three. Here we go, out for a fire drill in the middle of the night.''

Algie, stumbling into his slippers, followed Judy downstairs without a word. At the door they met Horace.

''I didn't see anything—'' he began.

''Well, I smelled something,'' Judy interrupted. ''Look again, Horace! I think there's a fire on the roof.''

All eyes turned to the sloping roof of the unfinished house. It dipped from the high peak, in a slanting line, all the way to the porch which was still a skeleton of white beams and

studding. The line was broken only by the
small dormer window. A distant street lamp
illumined the building only faintly but, through
this faint light, Judy made out a tiny curl of
smoke escaping from a break in the roof.

"It is a fire!" she cried. "Run for Peter's
telephone, Horace! We may be able to get the
fire department in time——"

Horace was gone but, in an instant, he was
back again with Peter who had already seen the
smoke and sent in an alarm.

"Can't we find a ladder and do something
about this ourselves while we're waiting?" he
suggested. "The workmen must have had a
ladder."

"There's one in the back yard," Mrs. Piper
told him eagerly. "It's right next to the little
park I made for Algie's chicken."

Algie himself ran to point it out. But his
short legs could not keep up with the boys'
longer ones and Horace and Peter were there
ahead of him. They had just dragged the ladder
to a good position when the screech of the siren
sounded down the street.

"No use fussing with this thing," Horace
said, dropping the ladder, "when we've got
real firemen to help us."

Judy had heard that Roulsville had recently installed modern fire fighting apparatus. There was a new truck, a combination hook and ladder, and behind that came the fire chief in his red car with the bell clanging.

It took only a moment to raise the ladder from the truck to the roof of Mrs. Piper's little house. The hose was laid quickly too, but it was of no use until some way could be found to reach the fire.

"It's up there in the peak," the chief directed, "but you men will have to cut a hole in the roof to get at it."

"They're going to cut a hole in the roof!" little Algie screamed, his eyes wide as the firemen mounted the ladder.

"There's a fire up there," Judy explained, "and they're going to cut a hole in the roof so they can put it out."

The firemen hacked a moment with their axes when suddenly a shout was heard from the back of the roof where a third man was working. The first two leaped back, barely saving themselves from sliding off the roof as a tongue of flame shot up from the other side, lighting the sky with a weird, red glow.

"Golly! That was a close one!" ejaculated

Horace. "The fire must be worse around in back."

Everybody ran to see. On the roof, from this new angle, they could see a square opening, almost like a window. It was here the fire was raging.

"A perfect square!" Peter said in amazement.

"That is strange," Horace agreed. "They're getting more and more modern with their fire fighting equipment."

"I doubt if the equipment had much to do with this," Judy declared. "The next thing we'll be seeing red circles in the fire. Anyway, the flame isn't blue."

Mrs. Piper gave her a startled glance, but neither Peter nor Horace knew what she was talking about.

"Oh, look!" Algie cried. "The fire's getting bigger. The firemen made it bigger!"

Again Mrs. Piper glanced at Judy. Her glance said, "What shall I tell him?"

Judy smiled and moved closer to the little boy. "You see, Algie," she said, "the firemen didn't make the fire bigger. They just let it out of the roof so it wouldn't burn the whole inside of the house."

"They're smart, aren't they?" Algie puffed out his chest. "I think I'll be a fireman when I grow up."

With a sigh, Judy stepped back again to where Peter and Horace were watching. There was nothing much they could do except watch now that experienced fire fighters had the situation in hand. They saw the red square of flame. They heard the sizzling noise as water poured on it from the long hose. Now the square hole was filled with white steam.

"Gee! I'd like to be up there myself and get a good look at that hole," Peter remarked. "They've removed the shingles in one piece."

"They couldn't have done that," Horace objected. "They just made a neat job of the chopping. By the way, Peter, what did you find out about the radio program?"

"I couldn't get anything but dance music. I've sort of given up the radio idea."

"I didn't think that theory was much good. But did you happen to look at our roof on the way over to your office?" Judy asked.

"I looked at as much of it as I could see. I can assure you there were no horses on it. Come on, folks, let's go back in the house and see if the fire scared them away."

Mrs. Piper hesitated. "Are you sure it's quite safe?"

"How about it?" Peter called out to the chief.

"Sure. The fire's practically out. You may smell a little smoke in there, but not enough to bother your eyes. The fire didn't have a chance to break through the ceiling."

"Thank Heaven! Then no damage was done," breathed Mrs. Piper. "They've saved my precious house!"

"Peter saved it," Judy said softly. "We wouldn't have been in time if Peter hadn't telephoned."

Algie was already running up the plank that served as steps and across the skeleton of the porch. He stopped at the door and screamed, "There's a cat in here! Get out, bad cat! Get out of my house!"

"Wait, Algie!" Judy called in alarm. "Don't touch him. He's mine!" She turned to Peter and said tragically, "We forgot Blackberry."

"I thought he'd follow us. He always does."

"He's all right anyway," Horace assured them. "He's still on his cushion right where he's been all evening. That shows how much impression the fire made on him."

"He's a bad cat——"

"Algie!" Judy interrupted, her voice severe. "How would you like it if every time I saw your pet chicken I screamed out, 'He's a bad chicken!' I have a pet that I love every bit as much as you love Fluff. And I think maybe it hurts his feelings when you scold him like that. See how sad he looks."

"He does look sad," Algie agreed. "I won't scold him any more. Really, I won't. Judy, can't we go upstairs and see where the fire was?"

Judy laughed.

"It was on the roof. I'm afraid we can't go up there tonight. But maybe we'll look around in the morning after you've had some sleep."

"I'll go to bed then," the little fellow volunteered cheerfully and started up the stairs. He wasn't afraid now. As long as he knew what was going on and there were no secrets being kept from him he was as interested and excited as any little boy would be. There had been a fire. He had seen the trucks drive up and put it out. Now he knew just as much about it as any one. Maybe more. For the grown-ups were still puzzling about something downstairs. Who started the fire? Why, he knew that. He decided he'd better go back and tell them.

"The men on the horses started the fire and they were on the roof all the time. On the back of the roof," he explained importantly, "where you couldn't see them."

"I guess that's as good an explanation as any," Judy agreed as she tucked him back into bed.

When she returned to the living room the fire chief was there making out his report.

"If you'd told us about that trap door, lady," he was saying to Mrs. Piper, "we wouldn't have had to hack a hole in your roof. And I might as well warn you, it isn't a very good idea to store suff in a place that's meant merely for ventilation. The Lord only knows how you got it up there!"

"What does he mean?" Mrs. Piper asked, turning an appealing look to Judy.

"He means," Judy answered, "that we're just about to solve this whole mystery. A trap door! Good Heavens! How do you suppose it got there and what could have been in it?"

"Some kid's sand box was all I saw," the chief answered. "All of it but the sand went up with the fire."

CHAPTER XVII

THE MORNING AFTER

IF IT hadn't been so dark Judy would have insisted upon raising the ladder they had found beside Algie's chicken pen and climbing up to the roof that very night. As it was, she had to wait until morning.

Peter and Horace stayed awhile to make sure everything was all right and then went back to the office to sleep. The house was quiet now and Judy was so weary that even the thought of the morning's investigation could not keep her awake once she lay down again on the cot. She overslept disgracefully. Mrs. Piper and Algie had already eaten their breakfast when she awoke. The sun was shining through the side windows of the little house and there was not a trace of snow left on the ground.

"Why, it's just like any May morning," Judy said to herself in surprise. Then she smiled as she recalled the storm and all the exciting things that had happened directly after it. No wonder that it seemed surprising

160

to wake up and find things just as usual. No ghost horses. No mysterious fires. No freak snow and, best of all, no red circles to warn her of something more that was going to happen.

Over by the fireplace on the cushion where Judy had placed him the night before, Blackberry was still sleeping. Judy patted him once or twice while she was dressing. He wasn't purring as he usually did when he slept. And when she finally walked out toward the kitchen to fix her breakfast, he did not follow her.

"I'm a terrible sleepy head," Judy apologized to Mrs. Piper who stood beside the new, built-in kitchen cabinet measuring something into a bowl.

"We expected you to sleep. I would have slept later myself if Algie hadn't waked me. Anyway, it's only ten o'clock."

"Ten o'clock! Good Heavens!" Judy exclaimed. "I hope Peter didn't want me at the office."

"I shouldn't think he'd feel much like working himself after last night's excitement," Mrs. Piper said.

"Anyway," Judy remembered, "it's Saturday. There's never much to do on Saturday. That is, in the office. There's plenty to do here.

We're going to start a real investigation.''

"You'll want a nice breakfast then. I saved some cereal for you and there's fruit and milk. Or if you want to make yourself some coffee——''

"The milk's better for me," Judy decided. "Mother says I need it to put a little meat on my bones. But Dad thinks it's staying up late that keeps me so thin. Oh, dear! Why can't exciting things happen in the day time instead of always at night?''

"They wouldn't be quite so exciting and not half as mysterious if you could see everything.''

Judy looked up from her breakfast, suddenly aware that Mrs. Piper was talking like a different person this morning. The sad tone was gone from her voice.

"Mysteries must be good for you," she remarked, dipping the tip of her spoon into an orange she had just finished cutting into neat segments.

"You're what's good for me," Mrs. Piper countered. "You're teaching me things I never knew before—how to live and enjoy every minute of it even when things do go wrong. How to face things and not be afraid and how not to frighten Algie. But now while we're

talking of it, Judy, I want to ask you something.
How would you tell him—that his sister Clara
is in the hospital and may—and may die? That
she isn't at her aunt's at all and that she
wasn't there but that when I was so worried and
frightened I didn't want him to be worried and
frightened too and—and I didn't let him
know.''

Judy considered this a moment, sprinkling
sugar on her oatmeal while she thought.

''That's what you were trying to tell me before, isn't it?''

Mrs. Piper nodded.

''It is difficult,'' Judy agreed. ''But I'll try
and think of a way to tell him. Is his sister
well enough so we could go and see her? I
know children aren't allowed in the hospital.
But maybe my father could get a special pass.''

''With Algie screaming the way he does?''

''I'd make sure he didn't scream.''

''I think you could do it too, Judy. I'm beginning to think you can do almost anything.
You and Peter and that nice brother of yours
can surely clear up this mystery and after
that—when my husband comes home——''

Her voice trailed off but the dreamy look in
her eyes said the rest of what she had tried to

say in words. She was looking forward to happiness. But there was still a cloud in the sky. Her little girl was in the hospital and wasn't expected to live. What a terrible secret to have kept all this time in silence! Judy would have been so glad to have talked it all over and sympathized if only she had known.

"Is it the Farringdon hospital?" she asked. "My dad's on their staff, you know. Maybe he could help."

"But he has helped! And I can't tell you how grateful I am to Peter."

"He is fine, isn't he? If he hadn't turned in the alarm——"

"But I wasn't talking about the fire," Mrs. Piper objected. "I was talking about my little girl. I would have asked him about her last night but I didn't quite dare. It was so soon. He wouldn't have been able to tell."

"To tell—what?"

"If it helped. He rushed away so soon afterwards. He—" Judy's bewildered look stopped her. "But can it be you didn't know?"

"No," Judy said. "Whatever it was, I'm sure I didn't know. Peter, right now, is one of my mysteries."

A knock sounded on the door. It was the

same knock that had terrified Mrs. Piper the
night before but now she recognized it and
smiled.

"There's Peter now. You'd better go, Judy.
I just dipped my hands into the flour. We're
going to have cookies."

Judy glanced appealingly at her. But there
was no use asking her to finish her story now.
Peter wouldn't want to wait.

"Good morning, traveler," she greeted him.
"Sorry, no ghosts today and no mystery but
you."

"No ghosts? Too bad! Horace has just
cooked up a good ghost story for the paper
and we were depending on you to finish it.
Don't tell me you've been on the roof!"

"Indeed not! I just finished breakfast.
Ladies must eat, you know."

"And they must sleep. I figured out that was
why you weren't at the office. Horace took your
place but he was too much interested in his
ghost story to be much use. I kept telling him
we might better be doing things than writing
about them and that he couldn't finish the story
anyway until we'd tracked down this mystery.
But you know what it is trying to talk to Horace
when he has an idea."

"What was the idea, do you know?"

"A detective yarn in installments. And a true one at that! He says he can outsharp the real estate sharpers too and if it is that limerick singer playing ghost——"

"If it *was*, you mean. Nobody's playing ghost any more."

"There'll be some clues on the roof anyway," Peter declared. "And I can't wait to get my hands on that trap door."

"You'll have to wait a minute," Judy said, "while I give Blackberry his milk. I forgot him again and he's lost his pep and doesn't remind me."

Peter waited in the living room, stroking the cat, while Judy filled the saucer. She sat it down but Blackberry merely sniffed at it.

"You see, he's lost his appetite too."

Algie Piper appeared at the door. He had been out playing, looking for the tracks the firemen made in the yard and the "snake places" where they dragged the hose. Now he ran over to Blackberry.

"Do his feelings still hurt?" he asked.

"I don't know," Judy said. "I'm afraid poor Blackberry is sick and we'll have to take him to a doctor."

"Do doctors doctor cats?" he asked, wide-eyed.

"My father would, I'm sure. Oh, dear!" Judy sighed. "I don't know which to do. Shall we take Blackberry home and let Dad doctor him or shall we go ahead with this mystery?"

"Couldn't your daddy doctor come here?" Algie asked unexpectedly.

Judy tried not to seem surprised although she did catch her breath in one startled gasp. She glanced toward the kitchen but, apparently, Mrs. Piper had not heard him.

"Wait a minute and I'll see," she said and darted through the door.

In a moment she returned and Mrs. Piper was with her. They had a scheme between them. Perhaps people didn't usually call human doctors for cats but, in this instance, it was different. The important thing was that Algie wouldn't be afraid to have the doctor come for Blackberry. Judy went back to the office to call him and, incidentally, to rouse Horace out of his ghost story and remind him that she and Peter were waiting to explore the roof.

Dr. Bolton was at the hospital, her mother said, and so Judy called him there.

"This may seem funny, Dad," she told him over the wire, "but I want you to come to Roulsville and see what's the matter with Blackberry."

"Your cat? But, Judy girl, my patients come first. I can't take the time. Why don't you bring Blackberry home and let me look at him this evening?"

"Because I want you here—for a reason. There's a little boy here—Algie Piper—and he's scared to death of doctors and his mother thought if he saw a doctor taking care of a sick cat——"

"Algie Piper, did you say?"

"Yes. His sister is in the hospital but he doesn't know it. Maybe you could tell me how she is."

"But there's no Piper girl in this hospital."

"There must be," Judy insisted. "Her name is Clara Piper."

"There's my little patient, Clara Smith, but you know about her. She's really improving at last. After last night's transfusion she began to look more like herself. I can say definitely that she will get well. But her mother hasn't been in and so nobody at the hospital could tell her."

Judy thought a moment. Clara Smith?
Clara Piper? Could it be that the two little
girls were the same? Mrs. Piper had tried to
conceal so many things for fear of frightening
somebody. It was quite plausible that she had
registered her child at the hospital under an
assumed name.

"Dad, please come," Judy begged. "Mrs.
Piper needs you even more than I do. It may
be that she is your little patient's mother."

"Very well, if it's that important. I have a
call to make in Roulsville anyway. But I can't
be there until after four o'clock."

"He's coming!" Judy cried, putting down
the telephone and turning with a triumphant
smile to her brother who was using Peter's
desk as a foot rest while he gave his ghost
story a final once-over.

"What's that?" Horace asked, looking up a
bit dazedly.

"Wake up, sleepyhead!" Judy cried. "Dad's
coming at four o'clock and, in the meantime,
we'd better get busy or we won't have time to
explore that roof. You may have a real ghost
story to add to this one when we're through."

CHAPTER XVIII

ON THE ROOF

"GET hold of that ladder," Peter directed Horace as soon as he and Judy had returned. "Let's put ourselves safely up on the roof before anything else happens to stop us."

"May I go first?" Judy asked when the ladder was lifted.

"It's wobbly. One of us will have to stay on the ground and hold it."

The three of them looked at each other. Excitement, adventure, thrills awaited them on the roof. On the ground there was nothing. Which one would give up the exploration?

Judy herself did not think of giving it up. One of the boys would be gallant enough to do that. But when Peter said gruffly, "I'll stay below," she suddenly realized how selfish she had been.

"No, I will. I'll have to look out for Blackberry anyway, in case he gets worse."

"But Judy," Peter protested, "it wouldn't be a mystery without you."

"I'll tell you what," Horace decided, "I'll stay down here at the bottom of the ladder and write up another ghost story and you two yell down at me when anything exciting happens. Then I'll know what to say."

"Are you sure you'd like that?" Judy asked.

"Sure," he agreed. "I never did think much of high places anyway. They get me dizzy."

"Okay then, Judy, you're first."

She began to ascend. Peter waited until she had reached the top before he put his foot on the ladder.

"It's funny up here," Judy called. "I can see right into the bedroom through the dormer window."

"Better catch hold of it for support. The roof's slippery!"

"It'll be even more slippery on the other side where the trap door is. What a goose I was to wear these high-heeled white shoes!"

"You'll fall, sure as shooting. Take them off," Peter advised. "You can climb better in your stockings."

Judy grasped the window ledge and, with the other hand, removed her shoes and kicked them toward the ground. One shoe barely missed Horace's head.

"First report from above!" he yelled. "A lady's white shoe! How am I going to fit that into a ghost story?"

"The same way it fits my foot," Judy called back. "Hardly at all!"

Peter helped her the rest of the way up the roof and they stopped a moment to inspect the burned hole near the chimney. He touched the edge of it and a piece of shingle crumbled off in his hand.

"You're going to be as black as a chimney sweep," Judy complained.

"This is nothing to what I will be when we've gone through that trap door," Peter told her.

"How do you suppose you open it?"

"Don't know," Peter replied. "We have to find it first."

It fitted closely, wherever it was. There was no evidence of any door in the roof although the hole beside the chimney was almost large enough to crawl through. Peter tapped and Judy poked, but no door could they find. Judy tried to lift up a section of shingles that she felt sure must be the door and almost slipped off the roof.

"Hey! This won't do!" Peter cried, helping her back to a safer place. "The firemen had their hatchets to pry up the door. We can't expect to do as much with our bare hands.''

They looked at each other, puzzled. It was obvious that neither of them could crawl through a trap door they couldn't find. But there was a hole in the roof—a burned and chopped-in hole. Judy had an idea.

''I'm slim,'' she said. ''I'll lower myself into that hole by the chimney and maybe I'll be able to push up the trap door from underneath.''

''That burned hole?''

''I don't mind getting black. It's Saturday anyway and you know what Saturday means.''

''Bath day,'' joked Peter. ''Saturday and New Years. I always start the new year right with a nice hot bath and then wait until Christmas——''

''You look it,'' giggled Judy, pushing her hand against his face and leaving still another smudge. ''Well, here goes! I think it's about time we both started praying——''

''That you don't go through the ceiling. Look out, Judy! Put your foot on a solid beam. There isn't any floor up there.''

''Who ever thought of leaving a cubby hole like this for ventilation anyway?''

"I guess you did," Peter charged. "You designed the house."

"I didn't want the bedroom ceiling coming up to a point, did I? All houses are built this way unless they have an attic. I suppose the trap door was John's idea. Ouch!"

"What's the matter?"

"I slipped. Did it ever occur to you that I couldn't see down here without a flashlight?"

"Here, take mine." Peter pulled it from his pocket and handed it to her. "See anything now?"

"Plenty!" Judy exclaimed. "It looks like the beach at Coney Island. Sand and driftwood and everything."

"She's found the sand!" Judy heard Peter yell down to Horace.

"Yes, and I've found the trap door too. Watch out! I'm pushing it now."

There was no mystery about the trap door once Judy was inside the tiny attic. It had been built on purpose and was plainly a common-sense measure in case of fire. Four boards nailed together like a window frame showed Judy where it was, the moment she turned her flashlight in the right direction.

She pushed up against the blackened frame and closed her eyes to keep out the falling cinders.

"I've got it!" Peter called from above. "Good work, Judy! Now may I come in?"

"If there's room for two. You can't stand up. You'll bump your head."

Peter let himself down cautiously and looked around.

"There was a floor at that. Rather a crude floor and part of it's burned away. But it's solid. By golly, it's good and solid! You could keep a grand piano up here."

"Looks as if somebody had kept one." Judy picked up a piece of burned wood that did look something like the leg of a grand piano.

"Say! That must be the leg of the sand box the firemen were telling us about."

"Yes, and here's another leg. Or what's left of it. But a sand box, my dear Peter, doesn't begin to explain our mystery."

"No," he agreed, "it doesn't. But it looks as if the sand box was about all that had ever been up here."

"The workmen had a box something like this to mix their mortar——"

"But the mortar box didn't have legs. Say!

Maybe this was one of those spirit tables. You know, the kind mediums use in seances. Maybe it was dancing by itself.''

Peter guffawed. ''A likely theory, that!''

''It's as good as any you've thought of,'' she countered, ''though I haven't much faith in it myself. Unless the table was equipped with horses' legs it could hardly make the sound we heard.''

''Speaking of sounds,'' Peter said, ''what's that?''

Judy listened and now she could hear a distinct scratching, followed by a scraping noise as though someone were crawling over the roof. Peter was about to poke his head out and see who it was when a head was poked in instead.

''Horace!'' they both cried together with a long breath of relief. ''What are you doing up here? Playing ghost?''

''Sorry if I scared you,'' he apologized. ''I merely came up to retrieve the lady's shoe.''

''Goose! As if I could wear it up here. And one shoe at that! What did you do with the mate?''

''What did I do with it? It was you who hurled this missle at me. I never saw the mate.''

"It's probably sticking to the roof somewhere then," Judy said. "If it wasn't so crowded in here we'd invite you in."

"No thank you," Horace replied with mock disdain. "I prefer to remain *white*."

"Better keep away from that hole then!"

But Peter had warned him too late. The portion of the roof on which Horace was standing had already been pretty well burnt and his weight was too much for the weakened shingles. Horace, shoe and all, came crashing through into the mysterious, windowless attic that Judy and Peter had discovered just under the roof of Mrs. Piper's house.

Crash! And a yell that was half a laugh and half a scream.

"Are you hurt?" Judy cried at once.

"My feelings, that's all." Horace attempted to stand up and hurt his feeling still more by bumping his head—*crack!*—against the roof.

Suddenly all three of them were howling with laughter. They looked at each other's dirty faces and howled still harder. The round glow from the flashlight and the streak of sunshine that sifted through from the hole overhead made them look like three negro comedians under a spot light.

"Bet we could hire out to a minstrel show!"

"Or haunt a house. We could scare the living daylights out of any superstitious soul who happened to meet us in this rig-out."

"And my poor shoe!" Judy cried, holding it up. "It's as black as we are—and no mate to keep it company."

"By the way, Horace," Peter said more seriously, "how'd you get up here anyway? You were supposed to steady the ladder when we came down."

"Oh, I discovered a new method of approach, via the maple tree. Suppose we all go down that way and sample Mrs. Piper's cookies. I think I smell them."

"Mmmm! Hot cookies!" Peter smacked his lips.

"And while we're going down," Judy suggested, "suppose we look for my other shoe. I hardly want to go 'round all day in my stocking feet."

"Agreed! Come on, Peter. I'll lead the procession down the tree."

They descended with more haste than care and forgot to look for Judy's shoe until they were on the ground. Then the bright idea occurred to Horace that it might have caught in the branches of the maple tree and he scrambled up to look for it.

"I always knew Horace was part monkey," laughed Judy as she watched him climb.

"And he's the one that gets dizzy in high places. Look out!" Peter called. "You may get a sudden attack of *vertigo*—" He glanced at Judy. "See! I know all the medical terms, even if I'm not a doctor's daughter."

"And I know all the legal terms too," she laughed back, "even if I am only a lawyer's stenographer."

"Secretary, my dear. There's a vast difference."

"In salary?"

"Not yet. Have patience and some day I'll bring all my earnings home to the little wife."

She looked at him, decided he wasn't being serious and laughed back, "Wife or stenographer, you wouldn't own me with this dirty face. I can't see through the soot on my eyelashes. Give me your handkerchief."

She rubbed it across her forehead and both handkerchief and face changed color.

"Oh, Lord!" groaned Peter. "You're making it worse."

Horace joined them. The search for the shoe

was fruitless but he had discovered a beautiful beetle for his latest hobby, a collection of bright-colored bugs.

"You'll have us all in your bug house if this keeps up. Say!" Peter reminded them. "We're missing those hot cookies."

They all started for the house, still laughing and making puns. Mrs. Piper met them at the door.

"Did you discover anything?" she inquired soberly.

"Our expedition of discovery degenerated into a search for Judy's lost shoe," Horace began pompously.

"And we're all as dirty as pigs and half starved for cookies."

"I came to tell you—" Mrs. Piper hesitated, looked from one laughing face to the other and suddenly she couldn't say it.

"Blackberry!" Judy cried. "He's worse! I know it! I can tell by the way you're looking at me. Oh, Mrs. Piper! I'll never forgive myself if we went up there on the roof and fooled around and had a good time and let Blackberry die!"

CHAPTER XIX

"IT ISN'T as bad as that," Mrs. Piper tried to console Judy. "But I'm afraid he's a pretty sick cat. His breath is wheezy and I don't like the glassy look to his eyes."

Judy bent over her pet, tears streaming down her cheeks and marking her face until everybody would have laughed at her if they hadn't all felt so much like crying in sympathy.

"I've been tooking care of him," little Algie said. "But he won't be tooked care of any longer. His head flops. See?"

"Don't, Algie!"

"He's trying to be a good boy, aren't you, Algie darling?"

"I'm sorry I scolded him and hurt his feelings and made him sick. When's your daddy doctor coming, Judy?"

"Oh, dear," she sighed. "It'll be hours!"

"We have to do something in the meantime. I think I have some directions," Mrs. Piper

181

offered. "They were left over from the time we had that spotted dog. I think they came inside some flea soap or something. Anyway, they tell what to do for the common ailments of dogs and cats. I tucked the paper inside my pocketbook and, if I remember right, it's still there."

"Look and see, won't you?" Judy pleaded. "We must do something. He looks as if he's suffering. Oh, Blackberry, darling! Don't roll those eyes so!"

Horace had often told Judy she was silly over her cat but now his face was just as sympathetic as Peter's. Both boys had their handkerchiefs out. Horace blew his nose with a loud toot.

"Here are the directions," Mrs. Piper announced. "It says what to do for distemper. Do you suppose he's got distemper?"

"I don't know. But it's something awful! What does it say?"

"Oh, dear! It says there isn't any cure, but during convalescence——"

"Wait!" Peter interrupted. "Maybe it's convulsions. It says apply cold water to the head."

"I'm sure that would make him feel better."

Judy applied a little cold water to her own face while she was fixing the wet cloth. Horace and Peter, noting the improvement, followed her example. But this time they did not joke over it. Blackberry was sick, maybe dying. And Blackberry was almost like a person. A cloud hung over the whole house and even when the cat seemed to feel a little better they still spoke in hushed voices and watched the clock anxiously until Judy's father should come.

"I was thinking," Judy said after they had finished a quiet lunch at the kitchen table. The cookies for dessert were barely warm. "I was thinking that if you didn't mind too much, Mrs. Piper, I'd like to borrow your bath tub and your shoes if they'll fit me. I never found my other shoe. I guess Blackberry can spare me while I clean up some more."

"She cleans up after her lunch like a cat." Horace attempted the joke but nobody smiled.

"I'll sit with Blackberry," Algie said. "He likes me to pat him."

A refreshing bath would do her good, Judy thought, but instead she felt a vague tiredness over her whole body.

"I do too much," she told herself. "I ought to relax. Dad always says, 'Relax a minute,

Judy girl. Don't spend all your energy.' "

Judy had spent a great deal of it. Perhaps that was why she felt so utterly exhausted. Mrs. Piper wouldn't mind if she lay down a moment—across Algie's bed. The bed was soft and comfortable. Somewhere downstairs someone was clattering dishes, probably putting them away. Judy had dried them and left them on the table, not knowing where they belonged. Now their tinkling was like faint music. Judy stretched herself. Oh, dear! She did feel tired. She closed her eyes and forgot everything until the knocker on the front door told her it was four o'clock and her father was there.

'She sat up with the sudden wide-awakeness of somebody just roused from a deep sleep. There is always that moment of wide awake panic when you cross the edge of the dream world and come back to reality and, for a moment, Judy thought she couldn't have crossed it. Surely she must be dreaming, for the thing that she saw happening now simply couldn't be happening to her.

It had been strange enough when she had seen the red circles marked with nail points on the unfinished house. It had been doubly strange when she had seen them dotted in the snow. Mrs. Piper had even seen them in the fire and now Judy was seeing them—of all places—on her own arm!

Three circles as blood red as the dots on the snow were marked with little pricks, like nail marks, in the white flesh of Judy's arm. There they were! Her eyes were seeing them. But her mind kept telling her she couldn't be awake. Then, still on the edge of wakefulness, she seemed to see a picture out of some magazine or poster or remembered from some long ago film—the four horsemen! What were they? Judy tried to think. War! Famine! Disease! Death! They had come riding—riding, on pounding hoofs. The third horseman, Disease, had caught up with her. The red circle had struck! Oh, how terrible—terrible! She dug her fists into her eyes, still struggling to rouse herself out of this horrible nightmare.

Downstairs she could hear her father's voice. If, as she now thought, the red circle was not a secret order but a strange, new disease, he would be the one to tell her. Never had his voice been so comforting or his arms so strong as now when Judy ran into them and sobbed out her story.

"But Judy girl," Dr. Bolton protested gently, "you've let yourself be alarmed unnecessarily. This is a common ailment. Only half an hour ago I was treating another case and, oddly enough, this man had let himself be frightened by it too. He had his arms and face all wrapped up in bandages as if it were something to be ashamed of and the infection was getting worse instead of better. Sunlight and good clean air are the best cures in the world for an infection like this. Of course, dear girl, we'll help nature along with some soothing medicine."

"But what is it, Daddy? How did I get it? What are all these awful red circles?"

"My dear girl, I'm sure you must have heard me speak of patients who had ringworm.'

"Is that what it is?" gasped Judy.

"That and nothing else."

"But how did I get it? How do people get it anyway?"

"Usually from animals—horses, parrots, cats. Now I'll have a look at Blackberry."

Just as Dr. Bolton suspected, under the cat's black fur were tiny circles of red. Sometimes there was one. Sometimes there were two, one within another. They were dotted onto his skin like red pin pricks—like the nail marks on the unfinished house. Like the dots of red on the snow. Suddenly Judy became the master of her fears and began to use her head. Whoever posted those warnings knew of this infection. But how could any one have known? How could any one have done a thing like this?

"It was a little circle like this that started all the trouble with Clara," Mrs. Piper was saying. "I thought the dog had bitten her. I told Algie it was the dog's fault and that's why he hated poor Spottie so. For a while he hated all animals and then he got attached to his chicken. That's why I was so anxious to buy it for him even though we might have to do without food for the balance of the week. There was nothing in the house but some jelly I had bought for Clara, hoping to tempt her appetite, and flour enough for bread. We were doing without a great many things then because the allowance my husband sent wasn't enough for our living expenses and the hospital too. He might have sent more money if I had told him but I didn't dare. He's had a nervous breakdown. It was the strain of his work and the worry of losing almost everything we had and, on top of that, Clara's sickness. His nerves couldn't stand it. He's still at his mother's recovering. His mother is quieting person and I knew rest and freedom from worry was all he needed to make him well. That's why I gave my name at the hospital as Mrs. Smith. I was afraid somebody would call him at his mother's if Clara got worse and I didn't want him to know. I didn't want Algie to know either. I always had to pretend I was going somewhere else when I went to see Clara. I hated leaving Algie alone but usually I had to. Remember that day I left him with you at the garden party, Judy? Visiting hours at the hospital were up at four o'clock and I hadn't seen Clara. She was worse that night and I stayed with her because I thought she was dying. That was the day they gave her the first transfusion. I can never thank Peter enough! Without his blood she never would have pulled through——"

Without whose blood? It was all confusing to Judy and, for a moment, she failed to grasp what Mrs. Piper was saying. Was Clara that little patient she had heard her father speak of so often? And had Peter given her his blood? But why hadn't she known about it before? She appealed to Peter himself.

"Was this supposed to be a secret?" she asked. "You've saved this little girl's life and yet you never told me!"

Peter blushed like a school boy. "I don't like people fussing over me and making a hero of me and, anyway, you were so mad over my breaking my appointment that you probably didn't listen to Miss Ames."

"So you told her and expected her to tell me?" Judy could not keep a trace of hurt pride out of the question.

"I certainly did. She promised to give you my message. She ran over to your booth and I supposed she did tell you. Naturally, she went back to the hospital with me."

"*Naturally.* Oh, Peter!" And Judy suddenly burst into tears and ran from the room.

Just outside the door she discovered Algie crouched in a corner. He had been listening to every word the doctor said. Now he knew his sister was in the hospital. Now he knew his mother had lied to keep him from being afraid. But Algie was dry-eyed and calm.

"You having a tantrum, Judy?" he asked as she ran past him.

She found his bed again and flung herself upon it, sobbing and shivering. This infection might be simple ringworm but it certainly made her feel awful. And on top of that, Peter! She wondered how she could ever stand it if he fell in love with that horrid, vulgar girl.

A step sounded on the stairs and Judy looked up. It was Peter.

"Judy, dear," he said, "you're sick. You ought to let your father take you home."

She felt her own forehead. It was hot and something inside it was throbbing and aching. He was right. Her thoughts got all mixed up when she was sick. She wouldn't think now. She would just have faith in Peter the way Honey had told her until things were straightened out and she understood.

While she was having her tantrum, as Algie called it, Dr. Bolton had been doctoring Blackberry with some ointment he had brought along in his satchel. The little boy was helping. All fear of doctors had left him the moment he knew the truth about his sister and realized that Dr. Bolton was helping make her well. The doctor won his heart still further by allowing him to help doctor the cat. But he was cautioned to wash his hands well in water mixed with a strong disinfectant. The others were all instructed as to its use so that they would not become infected too, and when the doctor had finished explaining it, Algie said, "Gee! You don't cut people up and stick needles in 'em. You're a funny doctor. You just make people wash their hands."

Blackberry was placed in a basket and the basket was set outside in the sun where nature and the healing medicine could do their work.

"He can ride in the car that way," Dr. Bolton said. "Better bring him home, Judy girl. You've caused these people trouble enough."

"The trouble was no trouble at all," Mrs. Piper assured him, "if Blackberry's being sick helps Judy find out who did this thing—who's responsible——"

"But nobody gives you ringworm on purpose."

"I'm not so sure of that," Judy said. "And Mrs. Piper's right about Blackberry. He always has helped us solve our mysteries and he may be helping us now in a way we can't understand. He's a brave cat, Blackberry is. Even when he's sick, he's sick for a reason."

"Coming with me, Judy girl?" the doctor

asked as he turned to go. "Better take Blackberry along in his basket and let your mother put you both to bed."

"Good idea!" Peter said.

"I have a few more calls to make. She might get home faster if you took her, Peter."

"Another good idea! Climb in, Judy. Blackberry's basket can ride on the back seat and you can snuggle down beside me. And don't think too hard on the way home."

But Judy had to think. She felt that now all the pieces to the puzzle were in her hands. The red circle was simply an infection. And it was caused by horses or parrots or cats. Horses! Parrots! Why, the limerick singer had bought a parrot and parrots made all sorts of noises. Why couldn't a parrot make a sound like running horses?

She told Peter her new theory and he thought as little of it as she did of his radio idea. But, lacking a better clue, he agreed to look up the parrot. An attempt to buy the bird would give them a chance to talk with the limerick singer anyway. And, once they talked with him, who could tell what surprising solution might develop?

CHAPTER XX

JUDY's arm healed more quickly than any one thought it would. By the middle of the following week the three circles had completely disappeared and, as no new circles appeared, the doctor told her it was quite safe to go about her daily work again.

Blackberry's skin took a little longer to heal.

"The disease is more serious with animals than with humans in most cases," Dr. Bolton explained.

Vigorous washings with the disinfectant were insisted upon whenever Judy touched her cat.

While she was confined to the house Judy had plenty of time to think things out. She remembered the other patient her father had spoken of and when she asked him she was not surprised to learn that this patient was John Olsen, her faithful carpenter. Her father had guessed the reason for the bandages.

"All those other workmen who were frightened by the red circle had this same infection and John was right, it does come silently and in the dark. Only," Judy thought with a smile, "mine came in the light right after I'd taken a hot bath."

But was the Red Circle explained so easily? Those sinister nail marks! Those blood-like drops on the snow! Judy felt more and more sure that somebody had had a hand in it. And who could it be if not the limerick singer who had purchased the parrot at the garden party?

As soon as she was well Peter accompanied her and they went to the offices of the Roulsville Development Company and inquired for the salesman who had the parrot. Judy gave his name, Al Allison.

"You'll find him at his house at this hour of the day," a young boy who was apparently not very familiar with the office rules, told her. It was still quite early in the morning.

"We'll have to be polite," Peter cautioned Judy as they approached the house. She noticed that it was a fine, modern building on a spacious plot of ground.

"Roulsville's proudest citizen! But he may not be so proud when we finish with him."

"Don't jump at conclusions, Judy."

"Now, Peter," she scolded him, "you're turning prig. Of course he knows something about this and of course the parrot——"

"Makes a noise like running horses. Of course," Peter agreed sarcastically.

They were almost quarreling about it when the limerick singer himself opened the door. Judy was polite—very polite. In fact, she was almost as polite as the limerick singer himself.

"I'm sorry to bother you, but I wanted to buy a parrot and I thought maybe that bird you bought at the garden party might be for sale if I offered a good price."

"That bird, my dear lady," the limerick singer replied with a smile and an unnecessary bow, "is not for sale. I will gladly give him to anybody who will take him off my hands."

"Indeed!" This was a surprise to Judy. "And may we take him off your hands, Mr. Allison?"

Al Allison forgot that he was supposed to be polite.

"Molly!" he shouted in to his housekeeper. "Get that good-for-nothing parrot and don't forget his cage! These people are willing to take him away."

"Praises be!" the woman replied, setting the cage with the parrot in it firmly outside the door.

Judy looked at Peter and Peter looked at Judy. Suddenly they both burst out laughing.

"All right. You're it! Make him trot like a horse."

"Aw, Peter! You do it. I don't know how."

"I have it!" Peter cried. "There goes the milkman! Maybe if he hears the milkman's horse he'll imitate it. Then we can tell."

They waited while the horse passed by, clop-clopping over the cement road. The parrot had his head cocked, listening.

"There goes your hat!" he croaked in an almost human voice.

"Well, can you beat that?"

"He hasn't forgotten. The mean old thing! That precious Miss Ames of yours had a hat just like mine at the garden party and that's what Scottie said to me."

"Why do you call her my precious Miss Ames?"

"Because you're so fond of her," Judy replied. "You broke appointments with me to go out with her and called her a poor little girl——"

Peter gasped. "Well, I never! Judy, it does take you a long while to get things through your head."

"Does it?"

"I should say. But if seeing is believing, as I always heard it was, you ought to understand the whole mess tomorrow when we take Algie to visit his sister at the hospital."

"I'll wait then," Judy promised. "We have to think up some way to make this visit pleasant for Algie so he won't be afraid. If he starts to scream in the hospital Dad will be blamed for issuing the pass. We can't have that."

"We can't have that," croaked the parrot. "We can't have that. We can't——"

"You're right," Judy agreed, throwing her jacket over his cage, "we can't have any more of your noise, Mr. Parrot. What a bright idea you turned out to be!"

"Get him home," Peter advised.

Judy laughed. "And I suppose you think that will solve the problem. I just hate to imagine the look on Mother's face when she sees this bird."

"Horace ought to be able to teach him some manners."

"You're right! I'll give him to Horace," Judy said determinedly as she set the cage down in the back of Peter's car.

Much to Judy's surprise, Horace was delighted with the arrangement. He felt sure the parrot would provide some clue to the mystery. "And if not," he added, "at least he'll be good company."

"You're welcome to his company," Judy replied, "as soon as Dad gets through with him."

The principal reason why she had bought the parrot was in order to take him to her father for an examination.

"If this parrot had ringworm," she explained, "he may have infected the workmen and he may have been left in the house for that very purpose."

"It's a good theory," the doctor agreed, handling the bird, "but you'll have to guess again, Judy girl. Do you see how fine and glossy this parrot's feathers are? They would be ragged and thin in places even if he had the infection some time ago and had now completely recovered. And there's certainly no evidence of infection. Keep him and Blackberry apart."

"I will," Judy promised. "You're going to

take us all to the hospital tomorrow, aren't
you, Dad? Maybe you could think of something nice that Algie could take to his sister.''

"She's still pretty sick. I can't think of
anything nicer than flowers. She isn't well
enough to play with toys.''

"I'll buy a big bunch of roses then. Algie
will like giving her roses.''

Judy bought the roses in Roulsville the following morning. She had her father stop on
purpose. Algie would like the idea of carrying
the flowers to the hospital himself.

"I haven't told him where he's going,'' Mrs.
Piper explained timidly when she met Judy at
the door of the same little house where all the
excitement had taken place only a week and a
half ago. The roof was fixed now and John
Olsen himself had done the work. He had also
heard the story of the red circle's further at-
tacks on Judy and her cat. But the red circle
had lost its terrors. Mrs. Piper said John
looked a little sheepish when she mentioned it.

"If only everything was that easy to explain,'' she sighed. "I'm worried sick about
this trip. If Algie ever screams——''

"But he won't,'' Judy interrupted gently.
"He knows about his sister already. He was

listening behind the door when you and my father were talking. But he's braver than you thought, Mrs. Piper. It's only your own fears that have frightened him.''

''I believe you're right. And I'm not afraid any longer. Oh, Judy! You're so good to us.'' And Mrs. Piper suddenly kissed her.

''I'm glad,'' was all Judy could say. Then she turned to Algie who had come running at the sound of her voice. ''Here are some roses for you,'' she said, thrusting them into his arms. ''I see you're all dressed up for Sunday just as you should be. But you're not going to Sunday School today. You're going to the hospital to see Clara. You may give the flowers to her if you like. I'm sure she'll love them.''

''B-but, but how are we going?'' the little fellow stammered. Judy could see he was thinking of ambulances and clanging bells and crowds of people with excited voices.

''We're going in Dad's car, just the same way I came here,'' she told him. ''Peter's going too. Hurry up, dear! They're both waiting.''

''Hurry up, Mommie! Get your hat on,'' Algie called. ''Judy's daddy doctor is taking us to see Clara.''

CHAPTER XXI

A TRAIL OF ROSES

ALL the way up the hospital steps, Algie dropped rose petals. Judy saw him doing it but said nothing. It wouldn't do to excite the little fellow now, and what did it matter if there were one or two roses less to give to Clara? There were two dozen in the bunch and she would never miss them.

"I can get out of here if I want to," Algie said at last in a whisper. Then Judy understood what he had been doing. If his mother went off and left him in the hospital he could follow the rose petals and find his way out. Judy had read him a fairy story where the lost childern followed a trail of rose petals and found their way out of the woods.

"Don't worry," she said, "your mother would never leave you here. She couldn't do without you, Algie."

A nurse in a white uniform showed them to a private room upstairs where a wan little girl

201

lay motionless on the bed. But she looked up when Mrs. Piper spoke to her and suddenly her face was wreathed in smiles.

"Roses!" she cried. "I've been hoping all this time that somebody would bring me roses."

"I brunged them," Algie said, forgetting how to talk properly in the excitement of seeing his sister again.

Clara looked at him, a little dismayed that they had brought him.

"You won't cry, will you?" she asked anxiously. "They'll put you out."

"I don't cry any more," he announced firmly. "I've growed up since you saw me."

Peter and Judy were standing by the door, afraid that too many visitors would excite Clara. But the little girl was a great deal better now and didn't want to leave anybody out of this nice little Sunday party she was having in her hospital room. She looked at them and smiled again. Clara's smile was something that not only curved her lips into a pretty bow. It glowed all over her face.

"I know who you are," she said. "You're Peter and Judy." She held out her hand to welcome them. "I've been wanting to know you. The nurse told me all about the nice big boy that gave me his blood in a funny bottle. Didn't it hurt when they took it out?"

"Not much," he answered, smiling back. "Not any more than it hurt you when they put it in again. And I guess you needed it more than I did."

"It didn't hurt at all when they put it in. It made me feel—good."

"Didn't they put it in with a needle?" Algie questioned anxiously.

"A needle's nothing," Clara told him. "You get used to it. You really get to like it when you know it's making you well. Dr. Bolton never hurts people without helping them too, does he, Judy? I may call you Judy, mayn't I?"

"Of course, dear. I wouldn't want you to call me anything else."

"Mommie's told me so much about you," Clara went on happily, "about the new house you had built for us in the town where Daddy's going to work. I'm going to get well in a hurry so I can see it."

"It's hardly more than a doll house," Judy explained. "We left room for it to grow." And, for ten minutes, she and Peter told the little girl about the house, speaking softly, so that she could rest while they were talking. Then Dr. Bolton came back. He had been making his rounds of the hospital while they visited and now he advised that Clara be left with her own family for a while.

"She's really not allowed more than two visitors at a time," he explained. "I only made this exception because I knew your visit would do her good and also, I thought my Judy girl would be a quieting influence on little Algie."

"He was like a little angel."

"Children are born imitators," the doctor said. "Being with so many other brave people was sure to give him courage and I mean Clara too. She's a little heroine, that child! In all my experience with children, I never had a better patient."

"And so polite!" Judy added. "I can understand Mrs. Piper's anxiety better than ever now. I suppose the whole family depended on her more than they realized and the thought of losing her— Why, I couldn't think of it myself if she were mine!"

"Shall we wait for Mrs. Piper?" Peter asked.

"I don't think it's necessary," the doctor replied. "I have to be here for a while anyway. I'll take her home."

"We'll follow Algie's trail of roses and get out of the woods then," laughed Judy. "Come on, Peter. The trail starts here at the top of the steps."

"Not so fast, Judy!" Peter cautioned her. "You'll get in the woods deeper than ever if you aren't careful. I thought we had another errand at the hospital. Seeing Clara wasn't the only thing we meant to do."

"But I don't understand——"

"I know you don't," Peter interrupted. "That's what I mean by being in the woods. But if we look around the hospital a bit before you go home, you may understand a lot of things."

"But I know this hospital by heart," Judy protested.

"You think you do. But I bet you haven't seen the new laboratory. You ought to see it. It's a honey!"

"We can't go in the laboratory, Peter. Dad never lets me go in. The laboratory's private."

"Not to me, it isn't," Peter said. "I've been

going there every Friday. That's where they take the blood out of me. You didn't think I sat by the patient's bed, did you? That's the old-fashioned way. In a modern hospital you just walk into the laboratory and an attendant sticks you with a needle and drains out the blood and carries it off in a glass tube. I never saw Clara Piper until today.''

"You didn't, Peter?"

"No. But I have seen the attendant. There she is now. You see, she's got a tray all ready to stick somebody else.''

The laboratory door was open now and a girl in white had just come through it. She was carrying a tray of bottles and test tubes and sterilized instruments and over half her face she wore the customary white mask. But Judy recognized her by her eyes.

"Miss Ames!" she gasped. "Peter! You never told me she worked in the hospital.''

"It never occurred to me until yesterday that you didn't know.''

"Miss Ames! Well, can you beat that! Dad's new laboratory assistant from New York and all the time it was Miss Ames and I never guessed it!''

Judy plopped herself down on a bench in the

hospital corridor. She thanked her lucky stars that she wasn't carrying the bottles and test tubes Miss Ames had on the tray, for surely she would have dropped them. To think that Miss Ames had been here all the time! She must have answered the telephone whenever Judy called her father at the laboratory. She must have answered it that day she called Peter!

"I bet you she's the girl who took that message you never got, Peter. I bet—" Miss Ames passed by them, eyeing Judy over her white mask.

"I wouldn't go in the laboratory now if I were you," she advised. "It might disturb somebody."

"That's all right," Peter agreed cheerfully. "We'll just sit here on the bench. I was showing Judy around but now I think she's seen everything I wanted her to see."

Miss Ames tossed her shoulders, jiggling the bottles as she walked on.

"She's high-hatting me today," Peter said, "because you're here. But she's glad enough to stick needles in me when I'm alone. She couldn't be nice enough to me that day at the garden party when she first told me the hospital needed me. She wanted me to hurry and insisted that I get the car out of its parking place while she ran back and told you."

"But she never told me anything. She never even spoke to me."

"I believe you, Judy," he declared. "She's the one who told me Arthur took you home that night you were stranded in Roulsville. That dame's had it in for me ever since we started fooling around with Mrs. Piper's house."

"She's in with the real estate people," Judy told him. "That's why. Remember how that parrot said, 'There goes your hat' the minute he saw me? Well, those hats were the cause of a big mistake that I would have told you about long ago if I hadn't thought you cared for Miss Ames."

"Cared for her? My eye! So that's what you thought!"

"You did speak of her affectionately, calling her a poor little girl——"

"You had me all mixed up," Peter interrupted. "The poor little girl was Clara Piper. When you said *that girl* I thought you meant Mrs. Piper's little girl and I couldn't understand why a sensible person like you would object to a fellow doing what was his plain

duty. Your dad called me up on the telephone.
You remember the call? And he called a lot of
other fellows he thought might be willing to
donate their blood. Mrs. Piper wasn't able to
pay anything and so he couldn't get a professional donor and there wasn't another one of
all those fellows he called in who had exactly
the right type of blood. He took the blood and
tested it, you see, and Miss Ames helped him.
Then when she told me my blood was the type
I couldn't get to the hospital fast enough. I
knew that Clara was expected to die but, of
course, I didn't know then that she was Mrs.
Piper's little girl. She was simply a nine year
old kid in need of help.''

"Oh, Peter!'' Judy cried. "And I quarreled
with you for that! What a beast you must
have thought me!''

"But why would Miss Ames cause such a
misunderstanding? It looks almost as if she
did it on purpose.''

"I think she did too,'' Judy agreed. "If she
had given me your message everything would
have been all right.''

"But what reason could she have had for not
giving you the message?''

"That's what I started to tell you, Peter—

about the hats. Miss Ames knew we were messing up the Roulsville Development Company's dishonest real estate racket so she tried to spoil our friendship on purpose. But it couldn't be spoiled that easily, could it?"

He squeezed her hand. "Not when we had faith in each other, Judy, and I kept on having faith in you."

"Forgive me, Peter. But if it hadn't been for Honey," Judy confessed, "I might not have had any faith in you at all. But Honey said I must depend on you and let things work out for themselves."

"And, thank Heaven, they're working out!"

"I guess they are," Judy agreed, "though it's still pretty puzzling. You say you left the garden party to go to the hospital laboratory with Miss Ames because she said you had the right type of blood for Clara's transfusion. But if she is a laboratory assistant, how can she be mixed up in real estate?"

"That's what I don't understand. But you were telling me something about the hats," Peter prompted her.

"Oh, yes. Some man—I couldn't see who he was—mistook me for Miss Ames and said, 'Look out for suckers.' That's how I first knew the game, Win-a-Lotto, must be a racket and that Miss Ames must know about it. I called you at the hospital. Dad said you were there helping him but he didn't say what you were doing. Well, I called you at the hospital and left a message for you to call me back and that it was something important. But you never called me. Now I think it was Miss Ames who took that message. She probably suspected what the call was about."

Peter agreed. "But what did you say to the man who mistook you for Miss Ames?"

"Oh, I made believe I was Miss Ames. I never looked at the man and so, of course, he couldn't see my face either. I just told him I would watch out for suckers."

"Clever Judy! That throws some light on a lot of things that have been puzzling me. It's so good to know you are the same Judy I always thought you were—clever and alert and quick-witted, but understanding too."

"I told you," Judy said softly, "that if we followed Algie's trail of roses it would lead us out of the woods."

"You were right," Peter agreed, taking her arm as they rose to go, "and both of us were in the woods deeper than we knew."

CHAPTER XXII

A CLUE AT LAST

THERE was a drug store right opposite the hospital and Peter suggested that they stop there for a soda before he took Judy home. There were still a great many things to talk over and so, instead of ordering the customary chocolate soda, Judy ordered a banana split that would take plenty of time to eat.

"You never told me what you found out about that parrot," Peter reminded her as soon as they had given their order. "He was supposed to be one of our best clues."

"I'm afraid the parrot disappointed us," Judy said. "He doesn't even say anything intelligent. Horace is trying to break him of calling people names but he hasn't had much success. He still yells, "You cheat!" at every good-looking man he sees. That was probably why the limerick singer wanted to get rid of him."

"No doubt it was," Peter agreed. "If we're right about his being mixed up in this real estate racket the parrot must have annoyed him considerably. But he may come in useful to us just the same. Some day we may want to accuse somebody of being a cheat and not quite dare say it. Then we can call in the parrot and watch the expression on the guilty person's face."

"That's an idea," Judy agreed with a giggle. "We might try it on the limerick singer himself."

"But we didn't buy the parrot for that purpose," Peter reminded her. "You were going to have your dad examine him and see if he could be the cause of this ringworm infection."

"Dad did examine him," Judy replied, "and he was sure he'd never had it."

"He is a disappointment then. But we still have something to work on. The infection could have been carried by some other animal."

"A horse, I suppose? But I still don't believe Blackberry was near any real horses and I never heard of a ghost carrying an infection."

"Say! That would be a headline for Horace's paper: GHOST HORSES CARRY

INFECTION TO CATS, DOGS AND PEOPLE.''

''Dogs, did you say?''

''I was thinking of that spotted dog,'' Peter said. ''He died, didn't he? He may have caught the infection too.''

''Caught it or carried it! Peter! The dog was there in the house right after that first warning was posted, *but before any of the workmen caught the sickness!* Blackberry was near him too. They fought each other the day before the dog died.''

''And there you have the whole thing in a nutshell,'' Peter agreed. ''I wonder why we never thought of the spotted dog before.''

''I guess it was because when Dad first told us about the infection he said it was caused by horses and parrots and cats. He forgot to mention dogs. But later when he and Mrs. Piper were talking about Clara he said her whole trouble probably started from a ringworm infection that wasn't properly taken care of. She thought the dog bit her but, instead, it might have given her ringworm. Dad said afterwards that dogs were active carriers.''

''That explains it all right,'' Peter agreed. ''Originally, the dog infected Clara Piper.

Then Mrs. Piper got rid of him without knowing he had anything the matter with him. But somebody knew! It must have been somebody familiar with such diseases and I can't help wondering if Miss Ames didn't have a hand in it. That somebody arranged to buy the dog at the garden party and either took him or had him taken to the workmen. He was left as a mascot, but you can see he was left on purpose.''

"I certainly can, because it was right afterwards that those other warnings about the red circle began to appear. We haven't found out how they were managed either. But it took some pretty clever planning to make them appear just as if they were something supernatural and appeared all by themselves. The red circles in the fire were just as strange, so Mrs. Piper says, as the red circles we saw in the snow. No wonder everybody was so frightened! I was pretty scared myself.''

"I'll say you were!" Peter put in. "I never saw you so upset by anything.''

"I'm like Algie," Judy confessed. "The things that frighten me the most are the things I don't understand. But we're beginning to understand a lot of things now, aren't we,

Peter? It looks as if the man who sold the workmen that spotted dog was at the bottom of all the trouble. Now if we can only trace him——''

"That ought to be easy," Peter interrupted. "He was probably the same man that bought the dog and, with your good memory of people's faces, you must know him by sight. If we can spot him among the Roulsville Development Company's men and you can identify him——''

"But I can't identify him," Judy cried. "I wasn't at the pet booth when the dog was sold. Scottie was. She's away at college now but we could send her a telegram."

"Let's do it then," Peter urged, taking a noisy suck at the last bit of his soda and rising to his feet.

"Hey, lady! Aren't you going to wait for that banana split you ordered?" the soda fountain clerk called after them as they hurried out of the door.

"I'll be back for it!" Judy promised. "Don't let it melt! I guess we can stow it away together," she told Peter. "I've lost my appetite for ice cream. All I crave now is a solution to this mystery."

At the telegraph office Judy found a yellow slip of paper and hastily wrote out this message to Scottie:

HAVE YOU ANY CLUE TO IDENTITY OF MAN WHO BOUGHT SPOTTED DOG IMPORTANT TRYING TO TRACE

"Do you think that will impress her?" she asked, handing the telegram to Peter for his inspection.

"I'll say it will. But suppose she hasn't any clue? Suppose she doesn't remember?"

Judy had considered that possibility before.

"But we can still ask John Olsen," she said. "Even if we can't identify the man who bought the spotted dog we can certainly find out who gave it to the men."

John Olsen was back at work again, this time really finishing the unfinished house. He had just completed the steps when Judy and Peter stopped to talk with him the following day. But he was finishing alone. His other men had never come back and it proved to be the two lazy brothers, the first to leave, who were responsible for the dog.

"They just had it here when I came in to work. They said a man gave it to them for a mascot but I doubted their word then and I do yet. They fooled around too much to be trusted anyhow and I can't say that I was sorry to see them quit.''

"Did they ever do any fooling around on the roof?'' Judy asked, her mind jumping to the conclusion that they might be responsible for the trap door.

"They did plenty of fooling around everywhere,'' John replied. "It wouldn't surprise me a bit if that real estate firm had them planted here on purpose to cause trouble. They came begging for work as soon as I agreed to build the house.''

"It's worth looking into,'' Peter agreed as he and Judy climbed into the car. They had just finished another day of hard work at the office and were on their way home. Peter's clients had been awarded their land by court decree the previous week and now they were coming back with questions about mortgages on the houses they meant to build. Peter referred them all to the Ace Building Company, Arthur's firm, and Arthur was glad to design a great many more tiny houses, similar to Mrs. Piper's, now that he knew the law was on his side.

"That's what I call outsharping the sharpers in a big way,'' Judy told Peter proudly.

"We're practically putting the Roulsville Development Company out of business."

"Merely putting them out of business isn't enough," Peter declared. "It leaves them free to start another swindling scheme somewhere else. But we'll do more than put them out of business if those workmen were infected on purpose. We'll put them behind bars where they belong."

"We could put them there for at least twenty years if we discovered they were responsible for that fire in Mrs. Piper's house," Judy said. "Chief of Police Kelly told me when we were investigating the school fire that the most serious of all offenses, short of murder itself, was setting fire to an inhabited dwelling by night."

"We're sure to pin some of these crimes on them," Peter agreed, "with all the new clues we've unearthed today."

But he and Judy were both due for a disappointment. A special delivery letter was waiting when Judy reached home but it merely said that Scottie had forgotten who bought the spotted dog. She hadn't the remotest idea what the man looked like. The only thing she did remember was the fact that Sylvia Weiss had cut a silhouette of him directly afterwards.

"It was a man anyway," Peter remarked, studying the letter for further clues after Judy had finished reading it.

"We might send a telegram to Sylvia," Judy offered dubiously.

"No use of that. She wouldn't remember either. But I'll tell you what we will do. Honey's art school is over the end of the week and she wants me to drive to New York and bring her home. Why don't you come too, Judy? We might stay a few days and do all the things we've always meant to do in New York and, incidentally, talk with Sylvia."

"Oh, I'd love that!" Judy cried. "We've worked hard and now that your clients have their real estate troubles all cleared up, we could do with a little vacation. Arthur's handling the building end of it and won't it be fun to come back to Roulsville and see how his model town has grown while we were away?"

"I'd feel safer about it if the Roulsville Development Company were out of business. But I guess we can chance it," Peter agreed. "We'll be gone only a week."

CHAPTER XXIII

JUDY's week in New York was brim full of excitement. There was something to do every day and Honey was so busy planning things that, at first, Judy hardly spoke of the mystery she and Peter were trying to solve. The excitement had almost crowded it out of her mind.

The three of them spent a day at Coney Island and bought tickets to steeplechase and rode down the make-believe race tracks on horses that went on wheels instead of hoofs. They rode the merry-go-round and the ferris wheel and went through the haunted mill. They ate hot dogs on rolls and frozen custard and French fried potatoes on tooth picks and all the other indigestible things people do eat at amusement parks. Then, the next day, they drove out to the acqueduct race track and saw the real races.

"Wherever I go," Judy said, "it seems I can't get away from horses."

"You have horses on your mind," Peter told

her, "because we never solved the mystery of those ghost horses in Mrs. Piper's house."

They told Honey all the things that had happened and now she was interested too. Neither she nor Judy knew much about race horses but both of them had an idea they made an enormous clattering sound, something like the sound Judy had described, as they ran around the track. But, although they stood by the wire netting right at the edge of the track and Judy could hear band music and people cheering and shouting, she could hear hardly a sound of horses' hoofs as they raced past her to the end of the stretch.

"Things are never the way you think they'll be," she complained. "It's no wonder we never understand half the noises we hear. I remember when I first went up in an airplane I imagined it would be all quiet and dreamy up above the clouds. But Arthur and I could hardly hear each other speak for the noise of the engine. And here I imagined the horses making a pounding noise with their hoofs the way they do when they race on the radio."

"That's what this modern age does to us," laughed Peter. "Everything is canned. Even our horse races."

"I wonder how they do it on the radio," Judy mused, a thoughtful expression on her face.

"I'm not sure myself," Honey put in. "But I know how you could find out. We haven't been to Radio City yet. Why couldn't we all go tomorrow morning and listen to a real broadcast?"

"Would they broadcast horse races?"

"I don't know about that. But you remember that fairy story program we always listened to, Judy? Remember how, in almost every story, the prince came on horse back? Well, your friend Irene Meredith knows the director of that program. Irene's been singing on the radio herself lately. I meant to write and tell you to listen. I'm sure she could get you the tickets."

The tickets for the program were easily secured. Irene and her husband, Dale Meredith the detective story writer, promised to accompany Judy and Peter and Honey to the broadcast. Dale would be a welcome addition to the party as he was always interested in Judy's methods of solving mysteries. Whenever she read one of his stories she discovered herself tracking down murderers and gangsters, sometimes in the guise of a boy, but always with her own unique methods. But, so long as he was interested in helping solve her mysteries, Judy didn't mind being Dale's story material. After he had heard all the details of her latest mystery he suggested, not only a trip to Radio City, but a party at his home with Sylvia Weiss as an invited guest.

"And don't give up your search for this man who bought the spotted dog," he advised. "Sylvia may know more about her silhouette customers than you realize. I happen to know that she cuts all her silhouettes on double thicknesses of black paper and saves a copy for her 'Scrapbook of Characters' as she calls it. Wherever she knows the person's name, she writes it down under his silhouette."

The program they wanted to hear did not go on the air until the following Saturday and so Irene and Dale planned to have their party first. Judy had made a number of friends on previous visits to New York and all these people were invited as well as some friends of Irene's that she wanted Judy to meet. They danced in the large living room of Irene's house which was a big, rambling place built a good many years ago when people expected

their homes to be converted, occasionally, into
ball rooms.   Tables for various games were
set up in an adjoining room and Sylvia brought
out her silhouettes, always an added attraction
at a party. There was a crowd around her at
first but when the novelty had worn off Judy
managed to have a little time with her alone.

"You may not know it," she announced,
"but you were asked here for a very special
reason. Of course," she hastened to add, "we
would have wanted you anyway, just for yourself. But it happens, Sylvia, that you have a
very important clue to a mystery Peter and I
are trying to solve. Do you mind if I look at
your scrapbook?"

"Why, of course not. It all sounds very in-
triguing. Do tell me about it," Sylvia urged.

It took quite a while to tell and while she
was reciting all the strange events of the past
few weeks, Judy was absently flipping the
pages of Sylvia's scrap book. Just as she had
supposed, Sylvia did not remember which
silhouette belonged to the man who had bought
the spotted dog.

"But I think," she added hopefully, "that
I would remember if you pointed it out to me."

So Judy looked more closely, trying to

recognize the limerick singer or that man with the bald head who had objected to her verse at the garden party or any one of the salesmen she had seen showing people the lots they had won. The names helped a little and she looked them over carefully, recognizing a great many Farringdon people, but nobody connected with real estate.

"Oh, dear!" she sighed. "If you'd only taken photographs of them."

"A silhouette would be just as easy to identify as a photograph," Sylvia said firmly. "Look through your garden party people once again and I'm almost sure you'll find it."

This time Judy studied the names more carefully than she did the pictures. Finally she found one labelled, "Mr. Ames."

"Is this it?" she asked, thrusting the book in Sylvia's hands. "This man looks familiar. He looks as though he might be the salesman who sold Mrs. Piper her house. He wouldn't give his name and so we called him "Mr. X.""

"Mr. X or Mr. Ames, he's the one," Sylvia cried out triumphantly. "I recognize that nose."

There was nothing else very distinguished about the man's appearance. But the nose was enough. It took a turn at the end, something like a parrot's beak.

"Your parrot was a clue at that," Judy called, running with the scrapbook to show Peter. "Only this parrot is a human one and his name is Mr. Ames."

Peter stopped dead still and stared at the silhouette. "Mr. Ames! Well I'll be shot for a swordfish if that isn't the same buzzard I've seen hanging around outside the hospital. He must be Miss Ames' brother—or her husband in case she wasn't Miss but Mrs. Ames. We've really hit on something at last, Judy! This bird is the responsible party. And it's easy to see where he got his tips. Miss Ames knew plenty about all of us. She knew Clara Piper's story from beginning to end and she could have easily told her husband or brother (whichever he was, about the dog with the ringworm. But I should think she would have had some pity for poor John Olsen, knowing how he suffers with asthma——"

"She knew that too?" Judy interrupted eagerly.

"Certainly she knew about his asthma," Peter replied. "She helped give him the skin tests. He didn't react to anything but rice powder and I remember how funny I thought it was when the interne who had charge of the case then suggested that John's wife use a different kind of powder on her face. That was the first Friday I was at the lab.''

"And he got a bad attack of asthma right after he started working on the house. Could Miss Ames have told this Mr. Ames or somebody else in this real estate gang and one of them sprinkled powder——''

"Suffering Cats! There was some white stuff on the floor that day, but I thought it was saw dust.''

"Sh!'' Judy cautioned him. ''Everybody's looking at you. Remember, we're still at Irene's party.''

"I don't care where we are,'' Peter declared fiercely. "This thing has gone far enough. The hospital ought to be told and Miss Ames ought to be dismissed before she causes any more trouble. We're taking no chances! You and Honey and I go back to Farringdon tomorrow morning.''

"But tomorrow morning's the broadcast,'' Judy protested. "We can't miss that.''

"Can't we though! We can always hear a broadcast. But it isn't always we can rout a

gang of crooks like this Roulsville Development gang. I tell you, we're wasting time here,
Judy. Miss Ames is in with this gang thicker
than gravy and the hospital ought to know it.''

"But what about the limerick singer?''
Sylvia Weiss put in timidly. "One of Irene's
friends was just telling me he used to know an
Al Allison who sang over the radio quite a
while ago. If you stayed for the broadcast
tomorrow you might be able to find out something about him too.''

Al Allison sang over the radio! Then she
and Peter were both right about that voice in
the attic. It was Al Allison's voice and the
voice of a radio singer too. If they kept this
up they'd soon be finding out the truth about
the horses.

"You see,'' she said, turning eagerly to
Peter. "He's in the gang too. There's no use
going this far in the investigation and then
turning back. We might as well go all the way.
Please, Peter! We are going to the broadcast
tomorrow morning, aren't we?''

"When you put it that way,'' Peter said, "I
don't see how I can very well stop us from
going.''

CHAPTER XXIV

THE FINAL ANSWER

THERE was no time to talk with any one at the studio the following morning. There was hardly time for a look at the beautiful buildings of which Radio City is composed. Irene herself was singing on an early program and not for anything in the world would Judy have missed hearing her friend's sweet voice being broadcast over the air. To her delight, she was allowed to go into the glassed-in sound room where all the directors were making motions with their hands and hear Irene's radio voice as well as her real voice singing into the microphone. Irene was indeed a Cinderella in the flesh, for once she had been only a poor mill worker in a Farringdon factory. But Judy, not a fairy godmother, had been responsible for the change. It was on her trip to New York with Judy that Irene met Dale Meredith.

The fairy story program went on the air directly after Irene's broadcast was finished.

Appropriately, the play scheduled for that morning was *Cinderella and the Glass Slipper*. It was acted out by children with the exception of the musicians and the man at the table. He was called "the sound effects man" and immediately Judy's interest centered upon him.

The room was suddenly hushed as the program began with a few strains of the familiar fairy tale music Judy had often heard on the radio at home. When it had faded away the children began talking, trying to decide how they should go to fairyland. It was all part of the play.

"Shall we go by plane or by boat or in a coach like Cinderella herself?"

"In a coach! In a coach!" a clamor of voices replied. "In a coach drawn by six white horses."

"Very well, then. A coach it is!"

This was the cue for the man at the sound effects table.

Clop! Clop! Clop! And away went the coach with its six white horses clop, clopping as noisily as ever the ghost horses raced in the tiny attic of Mrs. Piper's house.

Judy's eyes opened wide. The sound effects man had two half coconut shells with handles fixed on them and he was making the noise of galloping horses by simply pounding the coconut shells down, one after the other, in a box of sand. It was realistic enough. Over the radio you would think for sure that the studio must be filled with horses. Instead, there was a box of sand and two coconut shells. That was all. The noise was explained as easily as that.

Judy caught Peter looking at her, surprise in his face also, but she dared not to say anything now for the program was being broadcast and any noise she might make would be carried to the invisible audience over the radio. But the moment the program was over she said plenty and so did all the others. Who was this limerick singer? How would he get hold of a sound effects table? And where was this man Irene's friend had told them about—this man who used to know the Al Allison who sang over the radio?

In a studio in an adjoining building, they found the man and plied him with questions. Al Allison, it seemed, had once worked in that very studio. His story was a long, sad tale. But the tragedy was all of his own making. He had started out as a singer and had been

successful at first.   Audiences all over the
country became familiar with his singing, as
well as his speaking voice.   But success had
turned his head and before long he was placing
his own personal pleasures above the duty he
owed his public.   He came to the studio late,
often showing up after his program was all
over and they had been obliged to fill in with a
substitute.   Finally his director, growing tired
of his attitude, had given him the sound effects
table where, if he failed to show up, a substitute
could take his place without disappointing anybody.   But one day the limerick singer and
the table both failed to show up and, so far as
Irene's friend knew, nobody has seen Al Allison
since.   There was a rumor, though, that he was
singing limericks in some cheap burlesque
place.   But the disappearance of the table remained a mystery.

When the man had finished telling her all
this, Judy thanked him and, in turn, told him
her story.   He agreed with her that the limerick
singer was probably playing ghost with the
missing table and that when his efforts to
frighten the Piper family out of the house
failed, he had set fire to it.   Of course he was
doing it for money.   Al Allison had never been

known to play pranks on people just for fun.

"It's quite evident," the radio man said, "that he was what is commonly known as a professional ghost."

"I'm very anxious to prove that," Peter told him, "but we will need witnesses if we make charges against him and bring him to court. Our evidence up there in the attic is nothing but a few pieces of charred wood and a little sand."

"I'll be glad to testify," he replied, "if my story about the missing table will help."

"It certainly will. Thanks a thousand times. Now we must be on our way before our professional ghost thinks up any more pranks to play while we're gone."

All the way home Judy and Peter and Honey discussed what could be done, now that they had found out this much, about bringing the criminals to justice. First, it must be proved that Al Allison was employed by the Roulsville Development Company and that might be difficult. Then, even if there was evidence that he had stolen the table, it must be known that it was the limerick singer and not some other person hiding in Mrs. Piper's attic the day the roof caught fire. The charge would

be arson with a sentence of from twenty years
to life in prison. The district attorney would
not bring any such charge on guess work.

"I'm not sure enough of it myself to want
to see him sent up for that long time," Judy
confessed. "We could have been mistaken
about his voice and—and it was such a nice
voice. He was a sort of pleasant person."

"So was Miss Ames," Peter said grimly.
"But I'd be only too glad to see her sent up
for twenty years. She won't be, of course.
Even if we can prove that she and Mr. Ames
caused the spread of that ringworm infection
it would not be as serious a thing as setting fire
to a house at night. I feel a little discouraged
about it all, now that it's done. We haven't
enough evidence against any of them to impress the district attorney."

"Couldn't you handle the case yourself?"
Judy asked.

"Not yet," he replied. "I'm not important
enough for that yet. But if we go about this
thing sensibly, who knows? I may have a
chance to run for district attorney myself some
day. You'd vote for me, wouldn't you, Judy?"

She cuddled over beside him and pressed her
cheek against his coat.

"I'd vote for you for any office at all, Peter. There isn't anything I couldn't trust you to do. Honey was right about her brother. But I'm not sure I'd want you to be district attorney in Farringdon. Roulsville is beginning to seem like our town now that we're working there together. Your law office is there and I suppose you'll live there some day, won't you, Peter?"

"That depends on where you want to live, Angel."

"I'd be happy just anywhere," Judy said, "so long as the people I care about were there and I had something interesting to do and plenty of books and children around and, maybe, another mystery to solve."

"There'll always be a mystery," Peter told her gently, "the sweet mystery of life and if the way you've solved it for Algie Piper is any sample of the way you'll solve it for Peter Junior then I'll vote for you too. How would you like to run for the office of Mrs. Dobbs?"

"Tell him you'd love it," Honey broke in eagerly from the back seat. He had said this last in a louder voice and she knew he meant her to hear.

Judy sat straight again and looked at him

squarely. "How funny you talk, Peter. I'm not sure whether you're serious or not."

"You will be sure," he warned her, "when you're elected to the office. So just make up your mind to keep on liking Roulsville and maybe some day it will be our town."

"From what you've been telling me," Honey said anxiously, "I can't help wondering if the town will still be there."

"You're right, Honey," Judy agreed. "It won't be anybody's town if we don't hurry. The Roulsville Development Company won't give it to us without a fight and once they start fighting with fire . . . "

She left the sentence unfinished as the awful thought occurred to her that Roulsville could be swept away by fire just as it had once been swept away by flood. She glanced at the speed-ometer on the car, glad that the road was straight and that it was safe to drive as fast as she felt they must drive if they were to reach the town before it was too late.

CHAPTER XXV

THE MODEL TOWN

THEY made the trip in record time, stopping off only a minute in Farringdon to leave Honey with her grandparents and take Horace along in her place. Horace was a walking newspaper and they soon learned all there was to learn about everything that had happened while they were away. Their apprehensions were well founded. The fire department in Roulsville had been kept busy putting out small fires that were constantly starting, with no apparent cause, in the new houses the Ace Building Company was erecting for Peter's clients. Horace himself had asked that the employees of the Roulsville Development Company be watched and had cited his newspaper articles exposing their racket but so far nobody had been seen actually leaving one of the fires. None of them had done any great damage and there was a general belief that the workmen were careless with their cigarettes.

238

The information Judy and Peter had collected in New York was a great surprise to Horace. He was elated over their explanation of the ghost horses. A stolen sound effects table was just the climax he needed for the true detective yarn he was spinning for the Farringdon *Daily Herald*. He was even more positive than they were that the limerick singer was responsible for the fires.

"A fire bug is a man with an obsession," he declared, affecting the grand, know-it-all air that always annoyed Judy so. "If he will set one fire he will set a dozen. He does it because it is a mania and he can't help himself."

"He might not, by any chance, do it for money?"

"Well, whatever he does it for," Horace conceded doubtfully, "you ought to turn in your evidence at once. He can't set fires once he's safe in jail."

"You're right there," Judy agreed. "But the Roulsville Development Company can still pay somebody else to do it. What we want is to get together enough evidence to arrest the whole outfit as swindlers and conspirators. The police can deal with these separate charges after that."

"The district attorney is the man to see," Peter informed her. "His office is in the court house in Farringdon but, unfortunately, it isn't open until nine o'clock tomorrow morning."

Judy hardly slept that night. Visions of fires sweeping through her beloved Roulsville haunted her. Once or twice she woke up with a startled scream. But morning came at last and she and Peter were at the district attorney's office trying to persuade him to take action at once.

Judy knew her old friend, Chief of Police Kelly, would have listened to her. But Roulsville was out of his territory and so they had to depend on the district attorney. The charges or complaints, as he called them, had to be registered through his office anyway but, after listening to their story, he decided there was insufficient evidence to take action without first conducting an investigation. Payroll lists must be looked over and inquiries made as to the company's finances and all this must be done by the police before any arrests could be made.

"I suppose he's right," Judy agreed after they had left his office, "but it does seem a shame for him to pass all our evidence off so lightly. He says if we had proof that Al Allison had actually been in Mrs. Piper's attic at the time the fire started he'd consider having him arrested at once. But we haven't any real proof, have we, Peter? And he only laughed at the ghost horses.''

''It does sound silly, once you explain it,'' Peter agreed. ''But it's evidence enough if we had the table. Even if we had one of those coconuts he might consider it as proof.''

''But we never found out what the limerick singer did with the coconuts.''

''That's right. And there are a lot of other things we never found out. We don't know what made the circles in the fire and in the snow or who was responsible. We never even found that white shoe you lost the day we crawled up on the roof. What do you say we go back and look for it now?''

She agreed and, before the day was over, they also had a supper invitation from Mrs. Piper. Mr. Piper was home now and she wanted Judy to meet him. He looked much as she had supposed he would. He was a small, ineffectual individual who retired into himself a good deal and hadn't much to say at first.

The conversation at table was all about the new evidence Judy and Peter had collected in New York. Once more they explained the horses.

"We were hoping to be able to explain everything," Judy added, "but there are always a few mysteries in the world that nobody ever solves. Those red circles you saw in the fire appears to be one of them."

"What were you burning in the fire when you saw the circles?" Mr. Piper inquired unexpectedly.

"Rubbish, mostly," his wife replied. "Excelsior. Bits of wood. Broken off pieces of peach basket and some paper bags the workmen had carried their lunches in."

"Were the bags empty?"

"Well, I don't know that," Mrs. Piper confessed. "But I suppose they were. There wouldn't have been anything in them but scraps anyway."

"I was reading an article about fire at Mothers," her husband said, still in that thin, apologetic voice. "It mentioned the fact that rotting wood makes a grand fire display, almost like the Fourth of July. Of course, I don't know anything about solving mysteries and it's only an idea——"

"Ideas are all it takes!" Judy cried out enthusiastically. "Go on, Mr. Piper. What else did the article say?"

"It was all about different kinds of wood. It said cedar and pine were good for burning and dried orange peel makes a wondrous blue flame——"

"Dried orange peel! Say!" Peter interrupted excitedly. "Do you suppose there could have been some dried orange peel in those bags you and Mrs. Piper burned?"

"I was thinking that myself," Judy replied. "I told you the fire was blue with red circles in it, though I didn't see the red circles."

"We have some orange peels," Mrs. Piper offered. "I save them to grate for flavoring. Wouldn't it be fun to burn them and see what happens?"

Mr. Piper smiled at his wife's enthusiasm. It was something he had observed in her only lately and for which, had he known it, he could thank Judy and her flare for mysteries.

"Well," Judy laughed, "if you're willing to donate your orange peels to the cause, we might try it. If there were any orange peels in those paper bags you must have seen them when they first started to burn."

Mr. Piper had hit upon one solution even though he confessed to a complete ignorance of the technique of solving mysteries. Algie was delighted with the pretty fire and said he wished Clara could be home to see it.

"She'd like the rings. Look-ee! All the orange peels are burning in the middle first and the outside makes pretty red rings."

Clara would be home, his mother told him, in another week and Judy was glad it would be no sooner as the threat of fire still hung over Roulsville.

"There's one fire we can't lay at the door of the Roulsville Development Company," Peter remarked as the orange peels burned to embers. "I wonder if there is as simple an explanation as that to the red circles we saw in the snow."

"I was thinking," Judy said a lttle later when they were all out on the porch, now complete with its hammock and lattices, "I was thinking that if some one had a very long pole and had some small, circular thing attached to it he could easily stand on this porch roof and reach down with the pole and print circles on the snow. That is, if he had dipped the round things in red paint. He wouldn't leave any tracks then."

"Rather an elaborate performance, don't you think?" Mr. Piper remarked.

"And if you will remember," Peter put in, "there wasn't any roof on the porch when we saw those red circles in the snow."

"He could still have walked out on one of the beams."

But the others only laughed at Judy's theory. She'd have to think up something better than that. And then Peter suggested that she might have more luck figuring out the hiding place of her lost shoe.

"We'll leave you to figure it out by yourselves," Mrs. Piper said. "Come, Dow. You'll want to look at your paper and it's Algie's bed time. Come in when you feel like it, Judy. I thought you and Peter might like to enjoy the twilight here on the porch."

They looked at each other and then across the valley at the drowsy town. Lights were just beginning to twinkle and a misty haze was over everything. Through the haze they could see the partly finished houses that were being built for Peter's clients all along Judy Lane. Part of his dream had come true. The street was lined with attractive little doll houses something like Mrs. Piper's. He had spoiled the Roulsville Development Company's scheme and the model town was just as they had wished it to be except for the constant threat of fire.

"It seems impossible," Judy said, gazing thoughtfully at the twinkling lights. "The town is so peaceful now. Nothing could happen to break that peace."

But, as she said it, a new light appeared. This light was no twinkling electric bulb like the others. It was a tiny point of flame and it shot up from a pile of lumber just back of one of the tiny new houses. The black silhouette of a man could be seen running up the street.

"Now's our chance!" Peter cried, grabbing her hand. "We can head him off."

"That wouldn't be wise," Judy objected. "We've already seen what he did. The sensible thing would be for me to detain him here while you turn in a fire alarm and notify the police. Hurry, Peter, or he'll see you and suspect we're up to something."

Peter was out of sight before the limerick singer appeared, walking calmly now and looking perfectly innocent.

"Mr. Allison!" Judy called. "Do you have

a minute? You remember me from the garden party, don't you? I wanted you to look at a verse I wrote.''

He stopped and smiled his usual gracious smile. ''Oh, it's you, Miss Bolton? How's the parrot? I hope he isn't giving you trouble.''

''None at all,'' Judy assured him. ''I presented him to my brother and he's learning to quote newspaper headlines. But he still calls names,'' she added, trying to sound mournful. ''I don't believe we can break him of that.''

''You might try covering his cage with a blanket,'' the limerick singer suggested and Judy could not resist a little dig.

''Did it work when you tried it?''

''Not very well,'' he admitted. ''But let's look at the verse. I must be getting home. I expect they're waiting dinner.''

''I'll only be a moment. Do you mind stepping inside? I left the poem with Mrs. Piper. You might try one of her cookies while you're waiting. They're still warm.''

''I believe I will. Fire engines again,'' he remarked as the siren began screeching. ''Somebody in this town is always turning in false alarms.''

Judy glanced at him out of the corner of her

eye. She hadn't written any poem except the real estate limerick that he had already seen and she couldn't stall him off forever. But the fire engines were on their way. The police would soon follow and, sure enough, they arrived just as Peter came in, trespassing on the Roulsville Development Company's land as he ran around to the back door. Al Allison's escape was cut off. Two officers handcuffed him and took him away while he was still protesting his innocence. But the look he cast back at Judy proved his guilt to her beyond any possibility of doubt.

Up the street the sky was red with a new fire—all the proof anybody, even the district attorney, needed. For in the limerick singer's pockets the officers had found a quantity of matches. They had also found a queer little whistle just like the whistle they had used on the fairy story program when Cinderella's pumpkin was changed into a coach and the lizard into a coachman and six footmen appeared in place of six mice. The whistle, when the policeman blew it, made a sound as of something flying through the air. Judy and Peter both recognized it as the "ghost whistle" they had heard when the limerick singer had been hiding in the attic and trying to haunt Mrs. Piper's house.

"Well, that's done!" Peter remarked as he and Judy returned to the porch. "There'll be no more fires. They'll have the whole gang in for this. One of those officers just told me the district attorney had discovered Al Allison's name on the Roulsville Development Company's payrolls." He pressed Judy's arm as he said in a gentler tone, "Well, you can't say the town didn't need us. Is it our town, Angel. Or isn't it?"

"It's our town, Peter," she replied. "All ours. We're a couple of pioneers conquering a new wilderness. Isn't it wonderful to think we've saved it? It makes me feel good all over—like dancing a new step or doing something nobody ever did before."

"Marry me," Peter said. "Nobody ever did that before."

"Dear Peter!" she answered softly. "Perhaps I will."

But she knew he didn't like promises. She'd wait for the town to grow and make a place for them and in the meantime they would work and enjoy it together. She looked up, feeling romantic and hoping it was late enough for a moon. But instead of looking into the sky, she found herself looking into the branches of Mrs. Piper's maple tree.

"Do you see what I see?" she asked, nudging Peter. "Something white and it looks like the heel of my white shoe."

"Sure enough," he agreed. "I'll climb up and get it for you."

The shoe fell to the ground with a thud as Judy watched Peter remove something else from the hollow in the tree.

"Now do you feel sorry for the limerick singer?" he asked. "Now what do you think of our professional ghost who prints red circles in the snow without leaving any tracks? Is he getting what he deserves or isn't he?"

And Peter placed into Judy's arms the one missing link to their chain of evidence, a half coconut shell with a bit of tape tacked on for a handle. The tape looked as though it might have been tied about some long, thin object such as the pole Judy had mentioned. And all around the edges of the shell were bits of dried, red paint.

THE END

Printed in the United States
119364LV00005B/178-204/P